LANDO

LANDO

LOUIS L'AMOUR

BANTAM BOOKS
TORONTO · NEW YORK · LONDON · SYDNEY

LANDO

Bantam rack-size Book / December 1962
Louis L'Amour Hardcover Collection / March 1982

All rights reserved.
Copyright © 1962 by Bantam Books, Inc.

Book designed by Renée Gelman.

This book may not be reproduced in whole or in part,
by mimeograph or any other means,
without permission. For information address:
Bantam Books, Inc.

If you would be interested in receiving bookends for The
Louis L'Amour Collection, please write to this address for
information:

The Louis L'Amour Collection
Bantam Books
P.O. Box 956
Hicksville, New York 11801

ISBN 0-553-06214-X

Published simultaneously in the United States
and Canada

To
Ted McNulty
miner, bronc-rider, friend

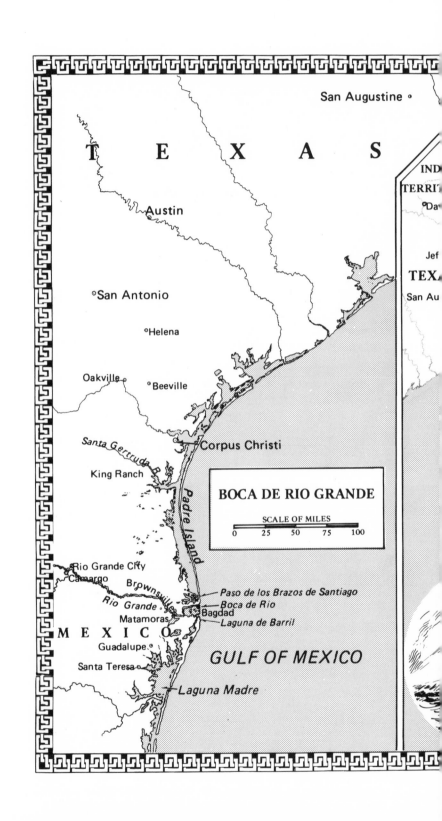

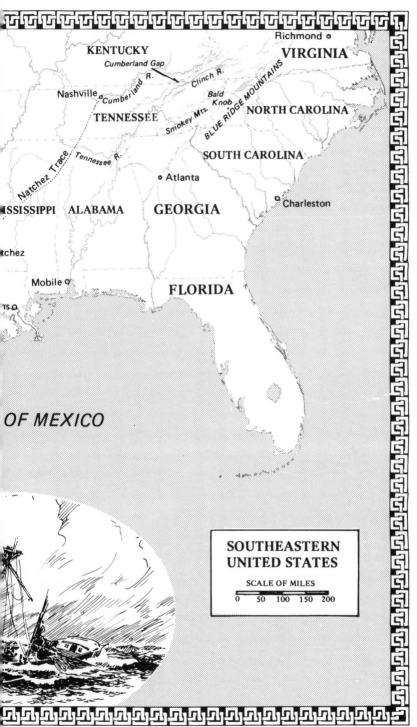

KENTUCKY

Richmond ○

VIRGINIA

Cumberland Gap

Cumberland R.

Clinch R.

Nashville ○ Cumberland R.

Bald Knob

Smokey Mts.

BLUE RIDGE MOUNTAINS

NORTH CAROLINA

TENNESSEE

Tennessee R.

Natchez Trace

SOUTH CAROLINA

○ Atlanta

SSISSIPPI ALABAMA GEORGIA

○ Charleston

tchez

Mobile ○

FLORIDA

ns ○

OF MEXICO

SOUTHEASTERN
UNITED STATES

SCALE OF MILES

0   50   100   150   200

Map by William and Alan McKnight

LANDO

ONE

We Sacketts were a mountain folk who ran long on boy children and gun-shooting, but not many of us were traveled men. And that was why I envied the Tinker.

When first I caught sight of him he was so far off I couldn't make him out, so I taken my rifle and hunkered down behind the woodpile, all set to get in the first shot if it proved to be a Higgins.

Soon as I realized who it was, I turned again to tightening my mill, for I was fresh out of meal and feeling hunger.

Everybody in the mountains knew the Tinker. He was a wandering man who tinkered with everything that needed fixing. He could repair a clock, sharpen a saw, make a wagon wheel, or shoe a horse.

Fact was, he could do almost anything a body could think of that needed doing, and he wandered up and down the mountains from Virginia to Georgia just a-fixing and a-doing. Along with it, he was a pack peddler.

He carried a pack would have put a crick in a squaw's

1

back, and when he fetched up to my cabin he slung it down and squatted on his heels beside it.

"If you reckoned I was a Higgins," he said, "you can put it out of mind. Your Cousin Tyrel cut his notch for the last Higgins months ago. You Sacketts done cleaned them out."

"Not this Sackett. I never shot 'ary a Higgins, although that's not to say I wouldn't had they come at me."

"Tyrel, him an' Orrin, they taken out for the western lands. Looks to me like you're to be the last of the Sacketts of Tennessee."

"Maybe I will and maybe I won't," said I, a-working at my mill. "I've given thought to the western lands myself, for a man might work his life away in these mountains, and nothing to show for it in the end."

The Tinker, he just sat there, not saying aye, yes, or no, but I could see he had something on his mind, and given time would have his say.

"You're the one has the good life," I said. "Always a-coming and a-going along the mountains and down to the Settlements."

There was a yearning in me to be off the mountain, for I'd lived too long in the high-up hills, knowing every twisty creek to its farthest reaches, and every lightning-struck tree for miles.

Other than my cabin, the only places I knew were the meetinghouse down to the Crossing where folks went of a Sunday, and the schoolhouse at Clinch's Creek where we went of a Saturday for the dancing and the fighting.

"Tinker," I said, "I've been biding my time until you came along, for come sunup it is in my mind to walk away from the mountains to the western lands."

Filling the mill's hopper, I gave the handles a testing turn, then added, "If you've a mind to, I'd like you to come with me."

Now, the Tinker was a solitary man. A long-jawed man, dark as any Indian, but of a different cast, somehow, and he'd an odd look to his yellow eyes. Some said he hailed from foreign lands, but I knew nothing of that, nor ought of the ways of foreign folk, but the Tinker knew things a body could scarcely ken, and held a canny knowledge of uncanny things.

Beside a fire of an evening his fingers worked a magic with rope or yarn, charming queer, decorative things that women took fancy to, but the likes of which none of us had ever seen.

"I have given it thought, 'Lando," he answered me, "but I am a lone man with no liking for company."

"So it is with me. But now it is in my mind to go to the western lands and there become rich with the things of this earth. You have the knack for the doing of things, and I have a knack for trade, and together we might do much that neither could do alone."

"Aye...you have a knack for trade, all right. A time or two you even had the better of me."

A time or two he said? *Every* time. And well he knew it, too, but it was not in me to bring that up.

"Except for one thing," I said. "You never would trade me a Tinker's knife."

He took out his pipe and settled to smoke, and I knew it was coming, this thing he had on his mind. "You have enemies. Is that why you have chosen to leave at this time?"

It ired me that he should think so, but I held my peace, and when I spoke at last, my voice was mild.

"Will Caffrey and his son? They have reason to fear me, and not I to fear them. It was my father's mistake to leave me with Will Caffrey to be reared by him, but pa was not himself from the grief that was on him, and in no condition for straight thinking."

"Caffrey had a good name then," the Tinker said, "although a hard-fisted man and close with money. Only since he became a rich man has he become overbearing."

"And it was the gold I claimed from him at Meeting that made him rich, and none of his earning. He had it from my father to pay for my keep and education."

"You put your mark upon his son."

3

"He asked it of me. He came at me, a-swinging of his fists."

When I had emptied the meal from the hopper, I tightened the mill and filled the hopper again, for such a mill as that of mine could grind only to a certain coarseness on the first grinding, and then the mill must be tightened and the meal reground before it was fit for the baking or for gruel.

"They are saying how you faced Will Caffrey at Meeting, and him a deacon of the church and all, and demanded he return the money your father left with him, and all the interest he had from its use.

"They tell how he flustered and would give you the lie, but all knew how five years ago you ran from his farm and have lived alone in this cabin since, and how, suddenly, after your father left Will Caffrey had money with which to buy farms and cattle.

"You'll not be forgiven this side of the grave, not by Will Caffrey. He is a proud man and you have shamed him at Meeting."

"The money is rightfully mine, Tinker. When he decided my father would not return, he took me from school and put me to work in the fields, and sent his son to school in my place."

The mill was ready, and again I ground my meal, the noise allowing for no talk, but when I'd emptied the hopper I said, "If it is enemies I have, it is the Caffreys. I know of no others."

He shot me a curious glance, which puzzled me with its content. "Not three tall, mustached men with dark hair and long faces? Three tall men as alike as peas in a pod...named Kurbishaw?"

"It was my mother's name."

"They are riding to kill you."

"You saw them where?"

"In the Cherokee towns. They asked questions there."

"The Indians are my friends. They will tell them nothing."

"When last I saw them they had old Midah Wolf and were buying him drink."

Midah was an old man with a love for the bottle and a memory of youth that only drink could bring back. When drunk, he was enemy to no man and would surely talk. He would be sorry after, but that would be of no help.

"The Kurbishaws are my mother's folk. They will surely be coming for other reasons."

"I have heard them say, 'We have killed the wolf, now we shall kill the whelp.'"

They had killed the wolf? If by that they meant my father, I did not believe them. My father might have many faults, but lack of shrewdness was not one of them. As I grew older I had remembered his actions around our mountain cabin, and now I knew that he had been aware of danger, that he had lived no moment without that awareness.

Yet he had not returned...had they killed him, indeed?

"I have only my father's worn-out rifle," I said, "and a dislike for shooting men I do not know, nor have I any appetite for violence."

The Tinker glanced at me shrewdly, and I wondered what went on behind those yellow eyes. Was he my friend, in truth? Had I learned this doubt of people? Was it acquired by brief but hard experience?

"If they find their way to the Crossing, Caffrey will be quick to tell them where you are." The Tinker turned his yellow eyes straight at me. "Did you never wonder why your pa came to this lonely place with his bride? There's a story told in the lowland towns."

"There was trouble when he married ma. Her family objected to him."

"Objected is a mild word. They objected so much they hired a man to kill him when his brothers-in-law decided against trying it. Your pa killed the man and then lit out for the hills so he would not have to kill her brothers and have their blood between them.

"Or so the story is told. Yet there is a whisper of something else, of something beyond pride of family. There is a tale that they hated your father for a reason before he even met your mother."

We Sacketts had come early to the mountains. Welsh folk we were, Welsh and Irish, and my family had come to America one hundred and fifty years before the Colonies fought for their independence. A relative of mine had been killed in the fierce fighting in North Carolina in the revolt that failed.

We settled on the frontier, as it then was, along the flanks of the Blue Ridge and Smoky mountains, and there we made ourselves part of the rocky hills and the forests. Pa was the first of our family to run off to the lowlands and return with a bride.

The Kurbishaws made much of themselves and cut a wide swath among the lowland folk, looking down their long noses at us who lived in the hills.

We Sacketts set store by kinfolk, but we never held up our family with pride. A mill grinds no corn with water that is past. Come trouble, we Sacketts stand shoulder to shoulder as long as need be, but we made no talk of ancestors, nor how high they stood in the community.

Yet it was no wonder that pa took the eye of the lowland girls, for he was a fine, upstanding man with a colorful way about him, and he cut quite a dash in the lowland towns.

He rode a fine black gelding, his pockets filled with gold washed from a creek the Cherokees showed him, and he dressed with an elegance and a taste for fine tailoring. There was gold from another source, too, and as a child I saw those hoarded coins a time or two.

My father showed me one of them and I loved the dull reflection of the nighttime firelight upon it. "There is more where that came from, laddie, more indeed. One day we shall gather it, you and I."

"Let it lie," ma said. "The earth is a fit place for it."

Such times pa would flash her that bright, quick smile of his and show her that hard light in his black eyes. "I might have told them where it was, had they acted differently about us," he would say; "but if they have it now it shall cost them blood."

How long since I had thought of that story? How long since I had even seen that gold until pa brought it out to turn over to Caffrey for my education and keep?

Her brothers had planned for ma to marry wealth and power, and when she ran off with pa they were furious, and challenged him. He refused them, and as he refused them he held two finely wrought pistols in his hands.

"You do not wish to fight me," he said, and tossed a bottle into the air. With one pistol he smashed the bottle, and with the second he hit a falling fragment. It was after that they hired a man to kill him.

Pa and ma would have lived their lives among the lowland folk had the Kurbishaws let them be, but they used their wealth and power to hound them out of Virginia and the Carolinas, until finally they took refuge in the mountain cabin among the peaks, which pa built with his own hands.

The cabin was a fair, kind place among the rocks and trees, with a cold spring at the back and a good fishing stream not a hundred yards off. And happily they lived there until ma died.

"If you stay here," the Tinker went on, "they will kill you. You have but the one barrel of your old rifle and they are three armed men, and skilled at killing."

"They are my uncles, after all."

"They are your enemies, and you are not your father. These men are fighters, and you are not."

My head came up angrily, for he spoke against my pride. "I can fight!"

Impatience was in his voice and attitude when he answered. "You have fought against boys or clumsy men. That is not fighting. Fighting is a skill to be learned. I saw you whip the three Lindsay boys, but any man with skill could have whipped you easily."

"There were three of them."

The Tinker knocked the ash from his pipe. "'Lando, you are strong, one of the strongest men I know, and surprising quick, but neither of these things makes you a fighter. Fighting is a craft, and it must be learned and practiced. Until you know how to fight with your head as well as with heart and muscle, you are no fighting man."

"And I suppose you know this craft?"

I spoke contemptuously, for the idea of the Tinker as a fighting man seemed to me laughable. He was long and thin, with nothing much to him.

"I know a dozen kinds. How to fight with the fists, the open hand, and Japanese- as well as Cornish-style wrestling. If we travel together, I will teach you."

Teach *me?* I bit my tongue on angry words, for my pride was sore hurt that he took me so lightly. Had I not, when only a boy, whipped Duncan Caffrey, and him two years older and twenty pounds heavier? And since then I'd whipped eight or nine more, men and boys; and at Clinch's Creek was I not cock of the walk? And he spoke of teaching *me!*

Opening his pack, the Tinker brought out a packet of coffee, for he carried real coffee and not the dried beans and chicory we mountain folk used. Without moving from where he was, he reached out and brought together chips, bark, and bits of twigs left from my wood-cutting and of them he made a fire.

He was a man who disliked the inside of places, craving the freeness of the open air about him. Some said it was because he must have been locked up once upon a time, but I paid no mind to gossip.

While he started the fire and put water on to boil, I went to a haunch of venison hanging in the shed and cut a healthy bait of it into thick slices for roasting at the fire. Then I returned to grind more meal.

Such mills as mine were scarce, and the corn I ground would be the last, for I planned to trade the mill for whatever it would bring as I passed out of the country.

If it was true the Kurbishaws sought to kill me they

could find me here, for mountains are never so big that a man is not known.

But the thought of leaving this place brought a twinge of regret, for all the memories of ma and pa concerned this place. Yonder was the first tree I'd climbed, and how high the lowest branch had seemed then! And nearby was the spring from which I proudly carried the first bucket of water I could hold clear of the ground.

No man cuts himself free of old ties without regret; even scenes of hardship and sadness possess the warmth of familiarity, and within each of us there is a love for the known. How many times at planting had my shovel turned this dark earth! How many times had I leaned against that tree, or marveled at the cunning with which pa had fitted the logs of our house, or put all the cabinets together with wooden pins!

The Tinker filled my plate and cup. "We shall talk of fighting another time."

Suddenly my quieter mood was gone and irritation came flooding back. No man wishes to be lightly taken, and I was young and strong, and filled with the pride of victories won.

"Talk of it now," I said belligerently, "and if you want to try me on, you've no cause to wait."

"You talk the fool!" he said impatiently. "I am your friend, and I doubt if you have another. Wait, and when you have taken your whipping, come to me and I will show you how it should be done."

Putting down the coffee cup, I got to my feet. "Show me," I said, "if you think you can."

With a pained expression on his lean, dark face he got slowly to his feet. "This may save you a beating, or I'd have no part of it. So come at me if you will."

He stood with his arms dangling, and suddenly I thought what a fool I was to force such a fight on a friend; but then my pride took command and my fingers clenched into a fist and I swung at him.

End it with a blow, I thought, and save him a bad beating. That was in my mind when I swung. Suddenly long fingers

9

caught my wrist with a strength I'd never have believed, and the next thing I knew I was flying through the air, to land with a thump on the hard ground. It fairly knocked the wind from me, and the nonsense from my brain as well; but then I saw him standing a few feet away, regarding me coolly.

Anger surged through me and I lunged up from the ground, prepared for that throw he had used upon me. This time I struck the ground even harder—he had thrown me in another way, and so suddenly and violently that I had no idea how it was done.

There was some sense in me after all, for I looked up at him and grinned. "At least you know a few tricks. Are these what you would show me?"

"These, and more," he said. "Now drink your coffee. It grows cold."

My anger was gone, and my good sense warned me that had he been my enemy I should now have been crippled or dead. For once down, he could put the boots to me and kick in my ribs, crush my chest or crush my skull. In such fighting there is no sportsmanship, for it is no game but is in deadly earnest, and men fight to win.

"Have you heard of Jem Mace?" he asked me.

"No."

"He was the world champion prize fighter, an Englishman and a gypsy. He whipped the best of them, and he was not a large man, but he was among the first to apply science to the art of fist fighting. He taught me boxing and I have sparred with him many times.

"Footwork is not mere dancing about. By footwork you can shift a man out of position to strike you effectively, and still leave yourself in position to strike him. By learning to duck and slip punches, you can work close to a man and still keep your hands free for punching. Certain blows automatically create openings for the blows to follow."

He refilled his cup. "A man who travels alone must look out for himself."

"You have your knives."

"Aye, but a hand properly used can be as dangerous as a knife." He was silent for a moment, and then added, "And a man is not lynched for what he does with his hands."

We both were still, letting the campfire warm our memories. What memories the Tinker had, what strange thoughts might come into his head, and of what strange things he had seen, I knew nothing, but my own memories went back to the day pa left me with Will Caffrey.

Three heavy sacks of gold he passed over to Caffrey that day, and then he said, "This is my son, of whom I have spoken. Care for him well, and every third coin is your own."

"You'll be leaving now?"

"Yes...to wander is a means to forgetting, and we were very close, my wife and I." He put his hand on my shoulder. "I'll come back, son. Do you be a good boy now."

Pa advised Caffrey to send me to the best schools and treat me well, and in due time he would return.

For the first year I was treated well enough, yet long before the change came I had seen shadows of it. Often at night I would hear Mrs. Caffrey complaining of the extra burden I was, and how much the money would mean to them if they had not to think of me. And Caffrey would speculate aloud on how much interest the money would bring, and what could be bought of lands and cattle with such an amount of gold.

Her words bothered me more than his, for I sensed an evil in her that was not in him. He was a greedy, selfish man, close with money and hard-fisted as well as self-righteous; but as for her—I think she would have murdered me. Indeed, I think it was in her mind to do so.

Caffrey had a reputation for honesty, but many a man with such a reputation simply has not been found out or tested, and for Will Caffrey the test of those bags of gold was too much for his principles to bear. The year after pa had gone they took me from school—their own son continued— and they put me to work with the field hands. Eleven years old I was then, and no place to go, nor anyone to turn to.

The day came when Duncan struck me.

Contemptuous of me he was, taking that from his parents' treatment of me, and he often sneered or cursed at me, but when he struck me we had at it, knuckle and skull.

It was even-up fighting until I realized all his blows were struck at my face, so I scrooched down as he rushed at me and struck him a mighty blow in the belly.

It taken his wind. He let go a grunt and his mouth dropped open, so I spread wide my legs and let go at his chin.

With his mouth open and jaw slack, a girl might have broken his jaw, and I did, for I was a naturally strong boy who had worked hard and done much running and climbing in the forest.

He fell back against the woodpile where I had been working, his face all white and strange-looking, but my blood was up and I swung a final fist against his nose, which broke, streaming blood over his lips and chin.

The door slammed and his ma and pa were coming at me, Will Caffrey with his cane lifted, and her with her fingers spread like claws.

I taken out.

So far as I could see, nothing was keeping me, and by the time I stopped running I was far off in the piney woods and nighttime a-coming on.

By that time I was twelve years old and knew only the mountains. The towns I feared, so it never occurred to me to leave all I had known behind.

The one place I knew was the cabin, and there I had known happiness, so I turned up through the woods, hunting the way.

It was thirty-odd miles of rough mountain and forest, and I slept three nights before I got there, the first nights I ever spent in the forest alone.

When at last I came to the cabin I was a tuckered-out boy.

If they ever came seeking me, I never knew. They might have come before I got back, or after, when I was off a-hunting. More than likely they were pleased to be free of me, for now they had the gold.

Five years I lived there alone.

That isn't to say I didn't see anybody in all that time. Long before ma died I used to go hunting with the Cherokee boys, and I could use a bow and arrow or set a snare as good as the best of them. These were wild Cherokees who took to the mountains when the government moved the Indians west.

Pa had been friendly with them, and they liked me. Whenever I was over that way I was sure of a meal, and many a time during that first year I made it a point.

Whilst working with Caffrey I had done most of the kitchen-garden planting, and there was seed at the house. The Cherokees were planting Indians, so I got more seed from them, and I spaded up garden space and planted melons, corn, potatoes, and suchlike. For the rest, I hunted the woods for game, berries, nuts, and roots.

It would be a lie to say I was brave, for of a night I was a scared boy, and more than once I cried myself to sleep, remembering ma and wishing pa would come home.

Those first years it was only the thought of pa coming back that kept me going. Caffrey had been sure pa was dead and had never left off telling me so, although why he should be so sure I never knew. It wasn't until I was past fifteen that I really gave up hope. In my thinking mind I was sure after that that he would not come back, but my ears pricked every time I heard a horse on the trail.

Travel was no kind thing those days, what with killers along the Natchez Trace and the Wilderness Road, Bald Knobbers, and varmints generally. Many a man who set out from home never got back, and who was to say what became of him?

First off, I swapped some dress goods ma had in her trunk for a buckskin hunting shirt and leggings; and after I had trapped, I traded my muskrat and red-fox skins with the Cherokees for things I needed. The cornmill was there, and after my first harvest I always had corn.

My fourteenth birthday came along and ma wasn't there to bake me a cake like she'd done, so I fried myself up a batch of turkey eggs. And that was a big day, because just shy of noon when I was fixing to set up to table, the Tinker came along the trail.

It was the first time I'd seen him, although I'd heard tell of him. He sat up to table with me and told me the news of the Settlements. After that he always stopped by.

The Tinker hadn't very much to say that first time, but he did a sight of looking and seeing. So I showed him around, proud of the cabin pa had built and the way he'd used water from the creek to irrigate the fields when they needed water— although rain usually took care of that.

The Tinker noticed everything, but it wasn't until a long time after, that some of his questions started coming back to mind to puzzle me. Especially, about the gold.

Once he asked me if I had any gold money...said he could get a lot for gold.

So I told him about all our gold going to Will Caffrey, and he got me to draw him a picture of what those gold pieces looked like.

"Your pa," he said, "must have been a traveled man."

"Sacketts haven't taken much to travel," I said, "although we hear tell that a long time ago, before they came over to the Colonies, some of them were sailors."

"Like your pa," he said.

"Pa? If he was a sailor he never said anything about it to me. Nor did ma ever speak of it."

He looked at a knot I had made in a piece of rope. "Good tight knot. Your pa teach you that?"

"Sure—that's a bowline. He taught me to tie knots before he taught me letters. Two half-hitches, bowline, bowline-on-a-bight, sheep's bend—all manner of knots."

"Sailor knots," the Tinker said.

"I wouldn't know. I expect a good knot is useful to a lot of folks beside sailors."

14

Aside from the cornmill and ma's trunk filled with fixings, there wasn't much left at the cabin beside pa's worn-out Ballard rifle and the garden tools. In the trunk was ma's keepsake box. It was four inches deep, four inches wide and eight inches long, and was made of teakwood. Inside she kept family papers and a few odds and ends of value to her.

The Ballard was old, and no gun to be taking to the western lands, so I figured to swap it off when I did the mill, or at the first good chance. If I was going to meet up with Bald Knobbers or wild Indians I would need a new, reliable gun.

Now the Tinker, he sat there smoking, and finally as the fire died down he said, "Daylight be all right for you?"

It was all right, so come daylight we taken off down the mountain for the last time.

One time, there on the trail, I stopped and looked back. There was a mist around the peaks, and the one that marked the cabin was hidden. The cabin was up there in those trees. I reckoned never to see it again, or ma's grave, out where pa dug it under the big pine.

A lot of me was staying behind, but I guess pa left a lot up there, too.

And then we rounded the last bend in the trail and my mountain was hidden from sight. Before us lay the Crossing, and I had seen the last of the place where I was born.

TWO

W e fetched up to the Crossing in a light spatter of rain, and I made a dicker with the storekeeper, swapping my cornmill for a one-eyed, spavined mare.

It was in my mind to become rich in the western lands, but a body does not become rich tomorrow without starting today, so I taken my mare to a meadow and staked her out on good grass. A man who wants to become rich had better start thinking of increase, and that mare could have a colt.

The Tinker was disgusted with me. "You bragged you'd a mind for swapping, but what can a man do with a one-eyed, spavined mare?"

Me, I just grinned at him. Two years now I'd had it in my mind to own that little mare. "Did you ever hear of the Highland Bay?"

"She was the talk of the mountains before she broke a leg and they had to shoot her."

"Seven or eight years ago the Highland Bay ran the legs off everything in these parts, and won many a race in the lowlands, too."

17

"I recall."

"Well, when I was working in the fields for Caffrey, the Highland Bay was running loose in the next pasture. A little scrub stallion tore down the fence and got to her."

"And you think this no-'count little mare is their get?"

"I know it. Fact is, I lent a hand at her birthing. Old Heywood, he who owned the Highland Bay, he was so mad he gave the colt to a field hand."

There was a thoughtful look in the Tinker's eyes. "So you have a one-eyed, spavined mare out of the Highland Bay by a scrub stallion. Now where are you?"

"I hear tell those Mexicans and Indians out west hold strong to racing. I figure to get me a mule that will outrun any horse they've got."

"Out of that mare?" he scoffed.

"Her get," I said. "She can have a colt, and sired by the right jack stud I reckon to turn up a fast mule."

We sat there on the bank watching that little mare feed on green meadow grass, and after a bit, I said to the Tinker, "When a man owes me, one way or another I figure to collect. Do you know where Caffrey keeps his prize jack?"

He didn't answer, but after a bit he said, "Nobody ever races a mule."

"Tinker, where there's something will run, there's somebody will bet on it. Why, right in these mountains you could get a bet on a fast cow, and many a mule is faster than a horse, although mighty few people believe it. The way I see it, the fewer folk who believe a mule can run, the better."

Caffrey's jackass could kill a man or a stallion, and had sired some of the best mules ever set foot. Before dark we were hidden in a clump of dogwood and willow right up against the Caffrey pasture fence.

The wind was across the pasture and from time to time the jack could catch scent of my mare, and while he couldn't quite locate her, he was stomping around in there, tossing his head and looking.

"Two things," I said, "had to work right for me to leave

18

this here country—the timing had to be right: You had to come up the trail, and that mare of mine had to be ready. And this here jack will work the charm."

"You're smarter than I thought," he said, and then we sat quiet, slapping mosquitoes and waiting until it was full dark. Crickets sang in the brush, and there was a pleasant smell of fresh-mown hay.

Watching the lights of that big white house Caffrey had built just two years ago, I got to thinking how elegant it must be behind those curtains. Would I ever live in a house like that? And have folks about who loved me? Or would I always be a-setting out in the dark, looking on?

Caffrey had done well with pa's money. He had it at a time when gold had great value, and he'd bought with a shrewd eye there at the war's last years. He was one of the richest men around.

When I called on him at Meeting to return the money I had no hope I would get it, but I wanted to put it square before the community that he had wrongfully used money with which he had been trusted. I'd no money nor witnesses to open an action for recovery...but almost everybody around had wondered where he got that gold money.

He had talked large of running for office, but I felt a man who would be dishonest with a boy was no man to trust with government. It always seemed to me that a man who would betray the trust of his fellow citizens is the lowest of all, and I wanted no such man as Will Caffrey to have that chance. When I called upon him at Meeting I had my plans made to leave the mountains, for now he would not rest until he had me jailed or done away with.

Right now I was risking everything, for if I was caught I would be in real trouble.

Slapping at a mosquito, I swore softly and the Tinker commented, "It's the salt. They like the salt in your blood. On jungle rivers mosquitoes will swarm around a white man before going near a native, because a white man uses more salt."

"You've been to the jungle?"

"I've heard tell," he said.

That was the Tinker's way. He would not speak of himself. Right then he was probably smiling at me in the dark, but all I could see was the glint of those gold earrings. Only man I ever did see who wore earrings.

His being there worried me some. He was an outlander, and Tinker or not, mountain folks are suspicious of outlanders. The Tinker was a needful man in the mountains, but folks had never rightly accepted him...so why had he come away with me?

When the barnyard noises ceased—the sounds of milking and doors slamming—we went up to the white rails of that fence and I taken a pick-head from my gear and pried loose that rail. That one, and the next.

The mare went into that pasture like she knew what she was there for, and against the sky we saw the jack's head come up and we heard him blow. Then we heard the preen and prance of his hoofs as he came toward the mare.

We waited under the dogwood, neither of us of a mind to get shot in another man's pasture. We were half dozing and a couple of hours had gone by. Even the mosquitoes were tiring.

Of a sudden the Tinker put a hand to my arm. "Somebody coming," he said, and I caught the flicker of the shine on a blade in his hand.

We listened...horses coming. Two, maybe three. The first voice we heard was Duncan Caffrey's.

"We've got to have a good horse or two in those races out west," he was saying. "The Bishop wouldn't like it if he lost money. The Bishop is touchy about money."

They had drawn up right beside the grove where we were hidden.

The older man spoke. "Now tell me about that gold. You say your pa had it from a man named Sackett? Where's that man now?"

"He left out of here. Pa thinks he's dead."

The Tinker cupped his hands to my ear. "Let's get out of this."

The trouble was that my mare was out in that pasture and I didn't want to leave her. No more did I want to leave off listening to that talk.

"You go ahead," I whispered. "I'll catch up or meet you at the crossing of the Tombigbee."

He hoisted his pack, then took up mine. How he disappeared so quick with those packs, I'll never guess. And at the time I thought nothing of his taking up my pack, for I'd have trouble getting it and the mare both out of there.

"What difference does it make?" Dun Caffrey sounded impatient. "He's nobody."

"You got it to learn," the other man said irritably. "You're a damn' fool, Dun. Falcon Sackett is one of the most dangerous men on earth, and to hear the Bishop talk about it, he's almighty important. So much so the Bishop has spent years hunting down every piece of that Spanish gold to find him."

"But he's dead!"

"You seen the body? Nothing else would convince the Bishop. I ain't so sure he'd even believe it then."

"Are you goin' to talk all night about a dead man? Let's go get the horses," and they moved on.

It was no use waiting any longer. If I was going to get away from here it had to be now. Stepping through the opening, I started out into that pasture after my mare and not feeling any too good about it, either. Jacks are a mean lot. If I was caught in the middle of this pasture by either the stud or the owner I might be lucky to get out alive.

It was almighty dark, and every step or two I'd hold up to listen. Once I thought I heard hoof-beats off to my left; but listening, I heard nothing more. Back behind me I heard rustling in the brush.

Suddenly, something nudged my elbow and there was

21

my mare. All day I'd been feeding her bits of a carrot or some turnips, so she found me her ownself. More than likely it was the first time anybody'd ever fussed over her.

Hoisting myself to her back, I turned her toward that opening in the fence.

The Bishop had been mentioned, and he was a known man. River-boat gambler, river pirate, and bad actor generally, he was one of the top men at Natchez-under-the-Hill, and one of the most feared men along the river.

"Whoever went in there," somebody said, "is still there."

A light glowed close to the ground as he spoke, then vanished.

Didn't seem no call to be wasting around, so I booted the mare in the ribs and she jumped like a deer and hit the ground running—and brother, she had plenty of scat.

She went through that fence opening and when a man reared up almost in front of her she hit him with her shoulder, knocking him rump over teakettle into the brush. The other man jumped to grab me and I stiff-legged him in the belly and heard the *ooof* as his breath left him. He went back and down out of sight, and the mare and me, we dusted around that clump of brush and off down the pike.

There was no need to meet the Tinker at the crossing of the Tombigbee, for I came up to him just as false dawn was spreading a lemon-yellow across the gray sky. He had stopped alongside the road and put both packs down. It looked to me like he was about to open mine when I came up to him.

"You got the wrong pack there," I said.

He turned sharp around, braced for trouble. He'd been so busy he'd not heard the mare coming in that soft dust. When he saw it was me he eased up and let go his hold on my pack.

"I was looking for the coffee," he said. "I thought you put it in your pack last night."

I didn't believe he thought anything of the kind, but I

was not going to argue with him. Only it started me thinking and trying to add together two and two, which is not always as easy as it seems.

"Take it from me," I advised, "and let's get back off the trail before we coffee-up. We may be sought after."

He pointed ahead. "There's an old trace runs up over the hills yonder. I was only down this way once, but I traveled it for a day or so."

Two days later I swapped my old Ballard for a two-wheeled cart. The Ballard wasn't much of a gun but I knew it so well I could make it shoot, and I let a farmer see me bark a squirrel with it. Now barking a squirrel is a neat trick, but most mountain boys could do it. A squirrel has little meat, and so's not to spoil any of it you don't shoot the squirrel, you shoot the branch he's setting on or one close by. It knocks him out of the tree, stuns him, and sometimes kills him with flying chips.

"You've a straight-shootin' gun," this farmer said to me. "Would you be of a mind to swap?"

We settled down to dicker. He was a whittler and a spitter, but I was natural-born to patience, so I waited him out. He was bound and determined to make a trade, and few folks came that way. That beat-up old cart hadn't been used in years, but the Tinker and me, we could fix it up. From now on we'd be in the flat-lands where it would be handy.

Between story-telling and talk of the Settlements, we dickered. We dickered again over hominy grits and sidemeat for supper, and we dickered at breakfast, but about that time I got awful busy making up my pack, talking to the Tinker and the like, and he began to think he'd lost me.

Upshot of it was, I let him have that Ballard and I taken the cart, three bushels of mighty fine apples, a worn-out scythe, and a couple of freshly tanned hides. The Tinker and me turned to and tightened the iron rims and the spokes, and loaded our gear.

It took two weeks of walking to reach the river, but by that time we had done a sight of swapping.

The little mare was looking good. Our daily marches were not long and the load she carried most of the way was light. We babied her along on carrots, turnips, slices of watermelon, and greens from along the road, and she fattened up on it.

We saw no sign of the three Kurbishaws, but they were never out of mind.

All the time I kept trying to dicker the Tinker out of one of his knives. He carried a dozen in his pack, and two belted at his waist. A third was slung down the back of his neck under his collar. They were perfectly balanced and the steel tempered to a hardness you wouldn't believe. We both shaved with them, they were that good. In the mountains a man would trade most anything for a Tinker-made knife.

Walking along like that, neither of us much to talk, I had time to think, and I remembered back to the Tinker asking about that gold. A man has a right to be interested in gold, but why that gold in particular? And Spanish gold, they said.

Why was the Tinker starting to open my pack? If he had found what he wanted, would he have made sure I didn't come up to him at the Tombigbee or anywhere?

Was it something about that gold that started the Kurbishaws after me?

I had no gold, and never had had any. So what did I have that they might want?

Nothing.

Nothing, unless maybe there was something in ma's keepsake box. The first time I was alone I'd go through that stuff of ma's again. I never had really looked at it—mostly, I kept it because it was all I had of hers.

All I had else was some worn-out clothes, some Indian blankets, and a couple of extra shirts.

Like I've said, walking gives a man time to think, and

a couple of things began to fit. Pa had never spent any of that gold that I could recall, but after Caffrey got it, some was spent. Not much right at first—he was afraid of pa coming back. And it was not long after Caffrey started to spend it that the Tinker showed up.

Not right away...it must have taken him some time to find out where that gold came from.

The Tinker was not a sociable man, but he had made a point of being my friend. He had spent time with me, and I believed he was really my friend, but I now believed he had some other interest in that gold.

That night we reached the Mississippi and the ferry. We were avoiding main-traveled roads, and the ferry we came up to was operated by a sour, evil-smelling old man who peered suspiciously at us. We dickered with him until he agreed to take us across for a bushel of apples.

He stared at our packs as if he was trying to see right through them, but mostly he looked at Tinker's knives. Neither of us had any other kind of a weapon, except that I carried a long stick to chase off mean dogs, of which we'd met a-plenty.

"Country's full of movers," the ferryman said. "Where might you folks be goin'?"

"Where folks don't ask questions," I told him.

He threw me a mean look. "Doubtless you've reason," he said. "We git lots of 'em don't want questions asked."

"Tinker, did you ever operate a ferry?"

"Not that I recall."

"I've got a feeling there's going to be a job open around here—unless somebody can swim with a knot on his head."

The ferryman shut up, but when we made shore near a cluster of miserable-looking shacks I thought I saw him make a signal to some rough-looking men loitering on the bank.

"Trouble," I said, low-voiced, to the Tinker.

A bearded man with a bottle in his hand, his pants held up by a piece of rope, started toward us. Several others followed.

The bearded man was big, and he was wearing a pistol, as were some of the others.

My walking staff was a handy weapon, if need be. A Welshman in the mountains had taught me the art of stick fighting, and I was ready.

The bearded man stopped in our path as we drove off the ferry. He glanced from the Tinker to me, and it was obvious that neither of us had a gun.

Four men behind him...a dirty, boozing lot, but armed and confident. My mouth was dry and my belly felt empty.

"Stoppin' around?"

"Passin' through," I said.

One end of my stick rested on my boot toe, ready to flip and thrust. A stick fighter never swings a wide blow—he thrusts or strikes with the end, and for the belly, the throat, or the eyes.

"Have a drink!" The big man thrust the bottle at the Tinker.

"Never touch it," the Tinker replied.

Two of the other men were closing in on me, about as close as I could afford for them to get.

"You'll drink and like it!" The big man suddenly swung with the bottle, but he was too slow. The Tinker's hand shot out, flicking this way and that as though brushing the big man with his fingers' ends, but the big man screamed and staggered back, his face streaming blood.

Even as he lifted the bottle, the two men nearest me jumped to get close. My stick barely had room, but the end caught the nearest man in the throat and he fell back gasping horribly. As he did so, without withdrawing the stick I struck sidewise with it, not a hard blow, but the other man threw up an arm to block it and staggered. Instantly I jerked back the stick, which was all of five feet long and broom-handle size, and grasping it with both hands, struck him in the face with the end of it.

The fight was over. The Tinker glanced at the other two men, who were withdrawing. Then he coolly leaned over and thrust the blade into the turf near the road to cleanse it of blood.

Three men were down and the fight gone out of the others, and it hadn't been twenty seconds since they stopped us. No doubt they'd robbed many a traveler at this point and believed us easily handled.

We paid them no more mind, starting off up the rise toward the high ground back of the river. And that big man was dead. From time to time I'd seen fighting done, but not a man killed before, and it seemed there ought to be more to it. One moment he was coming at us blustering and confident, and the next he was dying in the trail mud.

We did not stop that night, but went on, wanting distance between us and trouble. West and south we kept on going, through sunlight and rain, the Tinker plying his trade, and me swapping here and there.

The mare was filling out, carrying her colt, and I was in fine shape.

Down at Jefferson in Texas, we laid in supplies. We walked out of town before we made camp, and we were just setting up to eat when we heard horses soft-footing it along the trail.

Turning to warn the Tinker, I saw him standing outside the firelight, a blade in his hand.

Me, I held to my place at the fire, letting them think me alone.

The riders stopped out beyond the firelight and a voice called out, not loud, "Hello, the fire! Can we come in?"

"If you're friendly, you're welcome. Coffee's on."

Those days nobody rode right up to a fire or a house. It was customary to stop off a bit and call in—it was also a whole lot safer.

There were three of them, one about my own age, the other two a mite older. They were roughly dressed, like men who were living out in the brush, and they were heavily armed. These men, by the look of them, were on the dodge.

"'Light and set. We're peaceful folk."

27

They sat their horses, their eyes missing nothing, noting the Tinker there, knife in hand.

"You with the knife." The speaker was a handsome big man with a shock of dark, untrimmed hair. "You wishin' trouble?"

"Fixed for it. Not hunting it."

The big man swung down, keeping his horse between himself and the fire. "You look like movers," he said pleasantly. "I was a mover one time...moved to Texas from Tennessee." He gestured to the others. "These here are gen-u-ine Texans."

He hunkered down beside the fire as the others dismounted, and I passed him the coffee pot. He was wearing more pistols than I ever did see, most men being content with one. He had two belted on in holsters and a third shoved down in his waistband. Unless I was mistaken, he had another, smaller one in his coat pocket.

Loading a cap-and-ball pistol took time, so a man apt to need a lot of shooting often took to packing more than one gun. There was an outlaw up Missouri way who sometimes carried as many as six when on a raid. Others carried interchangeable cylinders so they could flip out an empty and replace it with a loaded one.

When the Tinker walked up to the fire they saw the other knives.

"You don't carry a pistol?"

"I can use these faster than any man can use a gun."

The youngest of them laughed. "You're saying that to the wrong man. Cullen here, he's learned to draw and fire in the same instant."

The Tinker glanced at the big man. "Are you Cullen Baker?"*

"That I am." He indicated the quiet-seeming man beside him. "This here's Bob Lee, and that's Bill Longley."

"I'm the Tinker, and this here is Orlando Sackett."

*The First Fast Draw, Bantam Books, 1959

"You're dark enough for an Indian," Cullen Baker said to the Tinker, "but you don't shape up to be one."

"I am a gypsy," Tinker said, and I looked around, surprised. I'd heard tell of gypsies, but never figured to know one. They were said to be a canny folk, wanderers and tinkerers, and he was all of that.

Cullen Baker and his friends were hungry, but they were also tired, and nigh to falling asleep while they ate.

"If you boys want to sleep," I said, "you just have at it. The Tinker and me will stand watch."

"You're borrowing trouble just to feed us," Bob Lee said. "We've stood out against the Carpetbag law, so Governor Davis's police are out after us."

"We're outcasts," Baker said.

"My people have been outcasts as long as the memory of man," the Tinker said.

"No Sackett," I said, "so far as I know, was ever an outlaw or an outcast. On the other hand, no Sackett ever turned a man from his fire. You're welcome to stop with us."

When they had stripped the gear from their horses the other two went back into the brush to sleep, avoiding the fire; but Cullen Baker lingered, drinking coffee.

"What started you west?" he asked.

"Why," I told him, "it was one of those old-timey gospel-shouters set me to considering it. He preached lively against sin. He was a stomper and a shouter, but a breast-beater and a whisperer, too.

"When he got right down to calling them to the Lord, he whispered and he pleaded, and right there he lost me. Seems if the Lord really wants a man it doesn't need all that fuss to get him worked up to it. If a man isn't ready for the Lord, then the Lord isn't ready for him, and it's a straight-forward proposition between man and God without any wringing of the hands or hell-fire shouting.

"When that preacher started his Bible-shouting and talking large about the sins of Sodom and Gomorrah, I was mighty taken with him. He seemed more familiar with the sins of those foreign places than he did with those of Richmond or Altanta, but mostly he was set against movers.

"Sinful folk, he said, and the Lord intended folks to stay to home, till the earth, and come to church of a Sunday. By moving, they set their feet on unrighteous paths.

"Fact was, he talked so much about sin that I got right interested, and figured to look into it. A man ought to know enough to make a choice; and pa, he always advised me to look to both sides of a proposition.

"Back in the hills mighty few folks ever got right down to bed-rock sinning. Here and there a body drank too much 'shine and took to fighting, but rarely did he covet his neighbor's wife up to doing anything about it, because his neighbor had a squirrel rifle.

"That parson ranted and raved about painted women, but when I looked around at Meeting it seemed to me a touch of paint here and there might brighten things up. He talked about the silks and satins of sin until he had me fairly a-sweating to see some of that there. Silks and satins can be almighty exciting to a man accustomed to homespun and calico. So it came on me to travel."

Baker cupped his hands around the bottom of his coffee cup, and taken his time with that coffee. So I asked him about that fast draw I'd heard them speak about.

"Studied it out by my ownself," he said. "Trouble is apt to come on a man sudden-like, and he needs a weapon quick to his hand. When Mr. Sam Colt invented his revolving pistol he done us all a favor.

"Best way is just to draw and fire. Don't aim...point your gun like you'd point your finger. You need practice to be good, and I worked on it eight or nine months before I had to use it. The less shooting you've done before, the better. Then you have to break the habit of aiming.

"It stands to reason. Just like you point your finger. How many times have you heard about some female woman grabbing up a pistol—something she maybe never had in her hands before—and plumb mad, she starts shooting and blasts

some man into doll rags. Nobody ever taught her to shoot—
she just pointed at what she was mad at and started blazing
away."

He reached inside his shirt and fetched out a gun. "This
I taken from a man who was troubling me—and you'll need
a gun in the western lands, so take it along. This here is a
Walch Navy, .36 caliber, and she fires twelve shots."

"*Twelve?* It looks like a six-shooter."

"Weighs about the same. See? Two triggers, two ham-
mers. She's a good pistol, but too complicated for me. Take
it along."

She was a mite over twelve inches long and weighed
just over two pounds, had checkered walnut grips, and was
a beautiful weapon. Stamped 1859, it looked to be in mint
condition.

"Thanks. I've been needing a weapon."

"Practice...practice drawing and pointing a long time
before you try firing. Don't try to aim. Just draw and point."

He put down his cup and got to his feet. "And one thing
more." He looked at me out of those hard green eyes. "You
wear one of those and you'll be expected to use it. When a
man starts packing a gun nobody figures he wears it just for
show."

Come daybreak, they saddled and rode away, and the
Tinker and me went west afoot. And as we walked, I tried
my hand with that gun. I practiced and practiced. A body
never knew when it would come in handy.

Somewhere behind me three Kurbishaws were riding to
kill me.

THREE

We were six months out of the piney woods of Tennessee when we walked into San Augustine, Texas. It was an old, old town.

Seemed like we'd never left home, for there were pines growing over the red clay hills, and everywhere we looked there were Cherokee roses.

We camped among the trees on the outskirts, and the Tinker set to work repairing a broken pistol I had taken in trade. An old man stopped by to watch. "Shy of gunsmiths hereabouts," he said. "A man could make a living."

"The Tinker can fix anything. Even clocks and suchlike."

"Old clock up at the Blount House—a fine piece. Ain't worked in some time."

The Tinker filled a cup and passed it across the fire to him, and the old man hunkered down to talk. "Town settled by Spanish men back around 1717. Built themselves a mission, they did, and then fifty, sixty years later when it seemed the Frenchies were going to move in, they built a fort.

"Been a likely place ever since. The Blount and Cartwright homes are every bit of thirty year old, and up until the War Between the States broke out we had us a going university right here in town."

He was sizing us up, making up his mind about us, and after a while he said, "If I was you boys I'd keep myself a fancy lookout. You're being sought after."

"Three tall men who look alike?"

"Uh-huh. Rode through town yestiddy. Right handy men, I'd say, come a difficulty."

"They're his uncles," the Tinker explained, "and they're all laid out to kill him."

"No worse fights than kinfolk's." The old man finished his coffee and stood up. "Notional man, m'self. Take to folks or I don't. You boys take care of yourselves."

The Tinker glanced over at me. "You wearing that gun?"

Pulling my coat back, I showed it to him, shoved down inside my pants behind my belt. "I ain't much on the shoot," I said, "but come trouble I'll have at it."

San Augustine was further south in Texas than I'd any notion of coming, but the Tinker insisted on it. "The biggest cow ranches are south," he said, "down along the Gulf coast, and some of them are fixing to trail cattle west to fresh grass, or north to the Kansas towns."

Now we'd come south and here the Kurbishaws were, almost as if they known where we were coming.

"No use asking for it," I said, "we'd better dust off down the pike."

"Didn't figure you would run from trouble," the old man said. "Best way is to hunt it down and have it out."

"They're still my uncles, and I never set eye on them. If they're fixing for trouble they'll have to bring it on themselves."

The old man bit off a chew of tobacco, regarded the plug from which he had bitten, and said, "You ain't goin' to dodge it. Those fellers want you bad. They offered a hundred dollars cash money for you. And they want you *dead*."

That was more actual money than a man might see in a year's time, and enough to set half the no-goods in Texas on my trail. Those Kurbishaws were sure lacking in family feeling. Well, if they wanted me they'd have to burn the stump and sift the ashes before they found me.

San Augustine was a pleasant place, but I wasn't about to get rich there. The mare was far along, but it would be a few weeks before she dropped her colt.

The Tinker started putting that pistol together and I went to rolling up my bed, such as it was. The Tinker said to the old man, "Isn't far to the Gulf, is it?"

"South, down the river."

The Tinker put the pistol away and started putting gear in the cart while I went for the mare. It was just as I was starting back that I heard him say, "This is the sort of place a man could retire...say a seafaring man."

The old man spat, squinting his eyes at the Tinker. "You thinkin' or askin'?"

"Why"—the Tinker smiled at him—"when it comes to that, I'm asking."

The old man indicated a road with a gesture of his head. "That road...maybe thirteen, fourteen mile. The Deckrow place."

We taken out with our fat little mare, and the cart painted with signs to advise that we sharpened knives, saws, and whatever.

We walked alongside, the Tinker with his gold earrings, black hat, and black homespun clothes, and me with a black hat, red shirt, buckskin coat, and black pants tucked into boots. Him with his knives and me with my pistol. We made us a sight to see.

Ten miles lay behind us when we came up to this girl on horseback, or rather, she came up to us. She was fourteen, I'd say, and pert. Her auburn hair hung around her shoulders and she had freckles scattered over her nose and cheekbones. She was a pretty youngster, but like I say, pert.

She looked at the Tinker and then at the sign on the wagon, and last she looked to me, her eyes taking their time with me and seeming to find nothing of much account.

"We have a clock that needs fixing," she said. "I am Marsha Deckrow."

The way she said it, you expected no less than a flourish of trumpets or a roll of drums, but until the old man mentioned them that morning I'd never heard tell of any Deckrows and wouldn't have paid it much mind if I had. But when we came to the house I figured that if means gave importance to a man, this one must cut some figure.

That was the biggest house I ever did see, setting back from the road with great old oaks and elms all about, and a plot of grass out front that must have been five or six acres. There was a winding drive up to the door, and there were orchards and fields, and stock grazing. The coachhouse was twice the size of the schoolhouse back at Clinch's.

"Are you a tinker?" she asked me.

"No, ma'am. I am Orlando Sackett, bound for the western lands."

"Oh?" Her nose tilted. "You're a *mover!*"

"Yes, ma'am," I said. "Most folks move at one time or another."

"A rolling stone gathers no moss," she said, nose in the air.

"Moss grows thickest on dead wood," I said, "and if you're repeating the thoughts of others, you might remember that 'a wandering bee gets the honey.'"

"*Movers!*" she sniffed.

"Looks like an old house," I said. "Must be the finest around here."

"It is," she said proudly. "It is the oldest place anywhere around. The Deckrows," she added, "came from *Virginia!*"

"Movers?" I asked.

She flashed an angry look at me and then paid me no mind. "The servants' entrance," she said to the Tinker, "is around to the side."

36

"You're talking to the wrong folks," I said, speaking before the Tinker could. "We aren't servants, and we don't figure to go in by the side door. We go in by the front door, or your clock won't be fixed."

The Tinker gave me an odd look, but he made no objection to my speaking up thataway. He said nothing at all, just waiting.

"I was addressing the Tinker," she replied coolly. "Just what is it that you do? Or do you do anything at all?"

One of the servants had come up to hold her stirrup and she got down from the saddle. "Mr. Tinker," she said sweetly, "will you come with me?" Then, without so much as glancing my way, she said, "You can wait...if you like."

When I looked up at that house I sobered down some. Here I was in a worn-out buckskin coat and homespun, dusty from too many roads, and my boots down at heel. I'd no business even talking to such a girl.

So I sat down on a rock beside the gravel drive and looked at my mare. "You hurry up," I said, "and have that colt. We'll show them."

Hearing footsteps on the gravel, I looked up to see a tall man coming toward me. His hair and mustaches were white, his skin dark as that of a Spanish man, his eyes the blackest I'd ever seen.

He was thin, but he looked wiry and strong, and whatever his age might be it hadn't reached to his eyes...or his mind.

He paused when he saw me, frowning a little as if something about me disturbed him. "Are you waiting for someone?" His voice had a ring to it, a sound like I'd heard in the voices of army officers.

"I travel with the Tinker," I said, "who's come to fix a clock, and that Miss Deckrow who lives here, she wanted me to come in by the servants' entrance, I'll be damned if I will."

There was a shadow of a smile around his lips, though he had a hard mouth. He taken out a long black cigar and clipped the end, then he put it between his teeth. "I am Jonas

Locklear, and Marsha's uncle. I can understand your feelings."

So I told him my name, and then for no reason I could think of, I told him about the mare and the colt she would have and some of my plans.

"Orlando Sackett...the name has a familiar sound." He looked at me thoughtfully. "There was a Sackett who married a Kurbishaw girl from Carolina."

"My father," I said.

"Oh? And where is he now?"

So I told him how ma died and pa taken off, leaving me with the Caffreys, and how I hadn't heard from pa since.

"I don't believe he's dead," I explained, "nor that those Kurbishaws killed him. He seemed to me a hard man to kill."

Jonas Locklear's mouth showed a wry smile. "I would say you judge well," he said. "Falcon Sackett was indeed a hard man to kill."

"You knew him?" I was surprised—and then right away I was no longer surprised. This was the Deckrow plantation, the place the Tinker had inquired about. At least, he had inquired about a seafaring man.

"I knew him well." He took the cigar from his mouth. "We were associated once, in a manner of speaking." He turned toward the door. "Come in, Mr. Sackett. Please come in."

"I am not welcome here," I said stiffly.

The way his face tightened showed him a man of quick temper. "You are *my* guest," he replied sharply. "And I say you are welcome. Come in, please."

Almost the first person I laid eyes on when we stepped through the door was Marsha Deckrow.

"Uncle Jonas," she said quickly, "that boy is with the Tinker."

"Marsha, Mr. Sackett is my guest. Will you please tell Peter that he will be staying for dinner? And the Tinker also."

She started to say something, but whatever it was, Jonas

38

Locklear gave her no time. "Peter must know at once, Marsha."

Nobody who ever heard that voice would doubt that it was accustomed to command—and to be obeyed.

"Yes, uncle."

Her backbone was ramrod stiff when she walked away, anger showing in every line of her slim figure. I wanted to smile, but I didn't. I kept my face straight.

Locklear beckoned me to follow and led the way into a wing of the house. The moment we passed through the tall doors I knew I had entered the rooms of a man of a very different kind from any I had known.

We went into a small hallway where, just inside the door, there hung on the wall a strange shield made of some kind of thick hide, and behind it two crossed spears. "Zulu—from South Africa," he said.

The large square, high-ceilinged room beyond was lined with books. On a table was a stone head, beautifully carved and polished. He noticed my attention and said, "It is very ancient—from Libya. Beautiful, is it not?"

"It is. I wish the Tinker could see it."

"He is a lover of beautiful things?"

"I was thinking more of the craft that went into it. The Tinker can do anything with his hands, and you should see his knives. We—we both shave with them."

"Fine steel." He rubbed out his cigar on a stone of the fireplace. "This tinker of yours—where is he from?"

"We came together from the mountains. He was a tinker and a pack peddler there."

When I had washed up in the bathroom I borrowed a whisk broom to brush some of the dust from my clothing, and when I got back to the library he was sitting there with a chart in his hands. When he put it down it rolled up so that I had no more chance to look at it.

He crossed to a sideboard and filled two wine glasses from a bottle. One of them he handed to me. "Madeira," he said, "the wine upon which this country was built. Washington drank it, so did Jefferson. Every slave ship from Africa brought casks of it ordered by the planters."

When we were seated and had tasted our wine, he said, "What are your plans, Mr. Sackett? You are going west, you said?"

"California, or somewhere west."

"It is a lovely land, this California. Once I thought to spend my days there, but strange things happen to a man, Mr. Sackett, strange things, indeed."

He looked at me sharply. "So you are the son of Falcon Sackett. You're not so tall as he was, but you have the shoulders." He tasted his wine again. "Did he ever speak to you of me?"

"No, sir. My father rarely talked of himself or his doings. Not even to my mother, I think."

"A wise man...a very wise man. Those who have not lived such a life could not be expected to understand it. He was not a tame man, your father. He was no sit-by-the-fire man, no molly-coddle. His name was Falcon, and he was well named."

He lighted another cigar. "He never talked to you of the Mexican War, then? Or of the man he helped to bury in the dunes of Padre Island?"

"No."

"And when he went away...did he leave anything with you? I mean, with you personally?"

"Nothing. A grip on the shoulder and some advice. I am afraid the grip lasted longer than the advice."

Locklear smiled, and then from somewhere in the house a bell sounded faintly. "Come, we will go in to dinner now, Mr. Sackett." He got to his feet. "I am afraid I must ask you to ignore any fancied slights—or intentional ones, Mr. Sackett.

"You see"—he paused—"this is my house. This is my plantation. Everything here is mine, but I was long away and when I returned my health was bad. My brother-in-law, Franklyn Deckrow, seems to have made an attempt to take command during my absence. He is not altogether pleased that I have returned."

He finished his wine and put down his glass. "Mr. Sackett, face a man with a gun or a sword, but beware of bookkeepers. They will destroy you, Sackett. They will destroy you."

At the door of the dining room we paused, and there for a minute I was ready to high-tail it out of there, for I'd eaten in no such room before. True, I'd heard ma speak of them, but I'd never imagined such a fine long table or such silver or glassware. Right then I blessed ma for teaching me to eat properly.

"Will the Tinker be here, sir?"

"It has been arranged."

Marsha swept into the library in a white gown, looking like a young princess. Her hair was all combed out and had a ribbon in it, and I declare, I never saw anything so pretty, or so mean.

She turned sharply away from me, her chin up, but that was nothing to the expression of distaste on her father's face when he looked up and down my shabby, trail-worn clothes.

He was short of medium height, with square shoulders and a thin nose. No man I had seen dressed more carefully than he, but there were lines of temper around his eyes and mouth, and a hollow look to his temples that I had learned to distrust.

"Really, Jonas," he said, "we are familiar with your habits and ways of life, but I scarcely think you should bring them here, in your own home, with your sisters and my niece present."

Jonas ignored him, just turning slightly to say, "Orlando Sackett, my brother-in-law, Franklyn Deckrow. When he would destroy a man he does it with red ink, not red blood, with a bookkeeper's pen, not a sword."

41

Before Deckrow could reply, two women came into the room. They were beautifully gowned, and lovely. "Mr. Sackett, my sister...Lily Anne Deckrow."

"My pleasure," I said, bowing a little.

She looked her surprise, but offered her hand. She was a slender, graceful young woman of not more than thirty, with a pleasant but rather drawn face.

"And my other sister...Virginia Locklear."

She was dark, and a beauty. She might have been twenty-four, and had the kind of a figure that no dress can conceal, and well she knew it.

Her lips were full, but not too full. Her eyes were dark and warm; there was some of the tempered steel in her that I had recognized in Jonas.

"Mr. Sackett," she asked, "would you take me in to dinner?"

Gin Locklear—for that was how she was known—had a gift for making a man feel important. Whether it was an art she had acquired, or something natural to her, I did not know, nor did it matter. She rested her hand upon my arm and no king could have felt better.

Then a Negro servant stepped to the door. "Mr. Cosmo Lengro!" he said, and I'll be damned if it wasn't the Tinker.

It was he, but a far different Tinker than any I had seen before this, for he wore a black tailored suit that was neatly pressed (he'd bribed a servant to attend to that for him) and a white ruffled shirt with a black string tie. His hair was combed carefully, his mustache trimmed. All in all, he was a dashing and romantic-looking man.

Jonas Locklear was within my range of vision when he turned and saw the Tinker. I swear he looked as if he'd been pin-stuck. He stiffened and his lips went tight, and for a moment I thought he was about to swear. And the Tinker wasn't looking at anybody but Jonas Locklear. I knew that stance...in an instant he could pick a steel blade to kill whatever stood before him.

The Tinker bowed from the hips. "After all these years, Captain!"

Virginia Locklear threw a quick, startled look at her brother, and Franklyn Deckrow's expression was tight, expectant. They were surprised, but no more than I was.

It was the first time I'd heard the Tinker's name, if that was indeed it, nor had I any idea he had that black suit in his pack, or that he could get himself up like that.

Jonas spoke to me without turning his head. "Were you a party to this? Did you know he knew me?" His tone was unfriendly, to say the least.

"I never even heard his right name before, nor have I known of anybody who knew him outside the mountains."

Not until we were seated did I again become conscious of my appearance. This table was no place for a buckskin hunting shirt, and Deckrow was probably right. I vowed then that this should not happen to me again.

That snip of a Marsha did not so much as glance my way, but Virginia Locklear made up for it. "Virginia does not suit me," she said, in reply to a question about her name. "Call me Gin. Jonas calls me that, and I prefer it."

The talk about the table was of things of which I knew nothing, and those who spoke might well have talked a foreign tongue for all the good it did me. Fortunately, I had never been one to speak much in company, for I'd seen all too little of it. I'd no need to be loose-tongued, so I held my silence and listened.

But Gin Locklear would not have it so. She turned to me and began asking me of my father, and then of the cabin where I had lived so long alone. So I told her of the forest and the game I had trapped, and how the Indians built their snares.

"Tell me about your father," she said finally. "I mean... *really* tell me about him."

It shamed me that I could say so little. I told her that he was a tall man, four inches taller than my five-ten, and powerful, thirty pounds heavier than my one hundred and eighty.

She looked at me thoughtfully. "I would not have believed you so tall."

"I am wide in the shoulders," I said. "My arms are not long, yet I can reach seventy-six inches—the extra breadth is in my shoulders. I am usually guessed to be shorter than I am.

"Pa," I went on, "was skillful with all sorts of weapons, with horses, too."

"He would be a man to know," she said thoughtfully. "I think I'd like to know him."

It was not in me to be jealous. She was older than me, and a beautiful woman as well, and I did not fancy myself as a man in whom beautiful women would be interested. I knew none of the things about which they seemed to interest themselves.

Yet, even while talking to Gin, I sensed the strange undercurrent of feeling at the table. At first I believed it was between Jonas and the Tinker, and there was something there, to be sure; but it was Franklyn Deckrow of whom I should have been thinking.

After dinner, we three—Locklear, the Tinker, and I—stood together in Locklear's quarters. Deckrow had disappeared somewhere, and the three of us faced each other. Suddenly all the guards were down.

"All right, Lengro," Locklear said sharply, "you have come here, and not by accident....Why?"

"Gold," the Tinker said simply. "It is a matter of gold, and we have waited too long."

"We?"

"In the old days we were not friends," the Tinker said quietly, "but all that is past. The gold is there, and we know it is there. I say we should drop old hatreds and join forces."

Jonas indicated me. "How much does he know?"

"Very little, I think, but his father knew everything. His father is the one man alive who knew where it was."

"And is he alive?"

"You," the Tinker said carefully, "might be able to answer that question. Is he alive?"

"If you suggest that I may have killed him, I can answer that. I did not. In fact, he is the one man I have known about whom I have had doubts—I might not be able to kill him."

"I don't know what you're talking about," I said, "but I am sure my father is alive—somewhere."

"You told me he planned to come back," the Tinker said. "Do you think he would purposely have stayed away?"

For a moment I considered that in the light of all I knew of him. A hard, dangerous man by all accounts, yet a loving and attentive father and husband. At home I had never heard his voice lifted in anger, had never seen a suggestion of violence from him.

"If he could come," I said, "he would come."

"Then he must be dead," the Tinker said reluctantly.

"Or prevented from returning," Jonas interposed dryly, "as I was for four years."

Far into the night we talked, and much became plain which I had not understood until then—why the Tinker had come to the mountains, and where he had come from; and why, when we reached Jefferson, he had insisted upon turning south instead of continuing on to the west.

I knew now that he had never intended going further west than Texas, and that he had thought of little else for nearly twenty years.

This was 1868 and the war with Mexico lay twenty years behind, but it was during that war that it all began.

Captain Jonas Locklear had sailed from New York bound for the Rio Grande with supplies and ammunition for the army of General Zachary Taylor. There the cargo would be transshipped to a river steamer and taken upstream nearly two hundred miles to Camargo. The Tinker had been bosun on the ship.

Captain Jonas had run a taut ship, respected but not liked by his crew—and that included the Tinker.

They had dropped the hook first off *El Paso de los Brazos*

45

de Santiago, the Pass of the Arms of St. James. From there orders took them south a few miles to *Boca del Rio,* the Mouth of the River—the Rio Grande.

It was there, on their first night at anchor, when all the crew were below asleep except the Captain and the Tinker, that Falcon Sackett emerged from the sea.

The Tinker was making a final check to be sure all gear was in place. The sea was calm, the sky clear. There was no sound anywhere except, occasionally, some sound of music from the cluster of miserable shacks and hovels that was the smugglers' town of Bagdad, on the Mexican side of the river.

Captain Jonas Locklear was wakeful, and he strolled slowly about the deck, enjoying the pleasant night air after the heat of the day.

Both of them heard the shots.

The first shot brought them up sharp, staring shoreward. They could see nothing but the low, dark line. More shots followed—the flash of one of them clearly visible, a good half-mile away.

Then there were shouts, arguments. These were dying down when they heard the sound of oars in oarlocks, and a boat pulled alongside.

There was a brief discussion in Spanish, the Tinker doing the talking. At that time Jonas knew very little Spanish, although later he learned a good deal. There was plenty of time to learn...in prison.

There were soldiers in the boat. They were looking for an escaped criminal, a renegade. As the boat started to pull away they backed on their oars and the officer in command called back. "There will be a reward...five hundred pesos...*alive!*"

"Whoever he is," the Tinker had said, "they want him badly, to pay that much. And they want him alive. He knows something, Captain."

"That he does," said a voice, speaking from the sea. And then an arm reached up, caught the chains, and pulled its owner from the dark water. He crouched there in the chains for a moment to catch his breath, then reached up and pulled himself to the top of the bowsprit, and came down to the deck. He was a big man, splendidly built, and naked to the waist as well as bare-footed.

"That I do, gentlemen," he had said quietly. "I know enough to make us all rich."

He was talking for his life, or at least for his freedom, and he knew he must catch their attention at once. There on the deck, the water dripping from him, he told them enough to convince them. And to his arguments he added one even more convincing—a Spanish gold piece, freshly minted.

By that time they were in the Captain's own cabin, a pot of coffee before them. The stranger dropped the gold coin on the table, then pushed it toward them with his forefinger. "Look at it," he said. "It's a pretty thing—and where that comes from, there's a million of them."

Not a million dollars—a million of such coins, each of them worth many dollars.

There in the cabin of the brig, the three men sat about the Captain's table—Jonas Locklear, the Tinker, and the man who was to become my father, Falcon Sackett. Jonas was the only one who was past twenty-five, but the story they heard that night was to effect a change in all their lives.

Thirty-odd years before, Jean LaFitte, pirate and slave trader, was beating north along the Gulf coast with two heavily laden treasure ships. During a gale one of these ships was driven ashore, its exact position unknown. LaFitte believed, or professed to believe, that the vessel had gone ashore on Padre Island, that very long, narrow island that parallels many miles of the Gulf coast of Texas. As a matter of fact, the ship had gone ashore some sixty miles south of Padre.

Six men, and six only, made it to shore. Of these, one died within a matter of hours of injuries sustained during the wreck, and a second was slain by roving Karankawa Indians while struggling through the brush just back from the shore.

The four who reached a settlement were more thirsty than wise. Staggering exhausted into the tiny village, rain-soaked and bedraggled, coming from out of nowhere, they hurried to the *cantina,* where they proceeded to get roaring drunk on the gold they carried in their pockets.

They woke up in prison.

The commandant at the village was both a greedy and a cruel man, and the four drunken sailors carried in their pockets more than three hundred dollars...a veritable fortune at that place and time.

Upon a coast where tales of buried treasure and lost galleons are absorbed with the milk of the mother, this gold could mean but one thing: the four sailors had stumbled upon such a treasure and could be, by one means or another, persuaded to tell its location.

The commandant had no idea with what kind of men he dealt, for the four were pirates and tough men, accustomed to hardship, pain, and cruelty. They were also realistic. They knew that as soon as the commandant knew what they knew, he would no longer have any need for them. They wanted the gold, and they wanted to live, and both these things were at stake. So they kept their secret well. They denied knowing anything of pirate treasure...they had won the money playing cards in Callao, in Peru.

Much of what they were asked could be denied with all honesty, for the commandant was positive they had stumbled upon gold long buried, and never suspected that they themselves might have brought the gold to the shores of Mexico.

Under the torture one man died, and the commandant grew frightened. If the others died, he might never learn their secret. Torture, then, was not the answer.

He would get them drunk. Under the influence, they would talk.

The trouble was, he underestimated their capacity, and overestimated that of himself and his guards. He judged their capacity by the effect of the first drinks, not realizing they had been taken on stomachs three days empty of food.

The result was that he got drunk, his guards got drunk, and the prisoners escaped. And before they escaped they cleaned out the pockets of the commandant and his guards, as well as the office strongbox (their own gold had been hidden elsewhere), and then they fled Mexico.

The border was close and they nearly killed their horses reaching it. Splashing across the Rio Grande, alternately wading or swimming, they arrived in Texas.

The year was 1816.

Texas was still Mexico, so they stole horses and headed northeast for Louisiana. En route one of the three men was killed by Indians, and now only two remained who knew exactly where the gold lay, and each was suspicious of the other.

Knowing where a treasure is, is one thing; going there to get it, quite another. Financing such a wildcat venture is always a problem; moreover, a "cover" is needed in the event the authorities ask what you are doing there. And there is always the question: who can be trusted?

Both men intended to go back at once, either together or each by himself, but neither could manage it. Both were out of funds, which meant work, and their work was on the sea. So they went to sea, on separate ships, and neither ever saw the other again. Each knew where there was a vast treasure in gold, but it lay upon a lonely coast where strangers were at once known as such, and the local commandant was greedy...and aware of the treasure's existence.

Then the year was 1846, and General Zachary Taylor had invaded northern Mexico and was winning victories, but was desperately in need of supplies. Steamboats were active on the Rio Grande, ferrying supplies across from the anchorage at Brazos de Santiago to the waiting steamboats at Boca del Rio. The steamboats that could navigate off the coast drew too much water for the river, so all goods must be transferred.

In command of one of those waiting boats was Captain Falcon Sackett.

The war with Mexico offered opportunity for any number of adventurers, outlaws, and ne'er-do-wells, who came at once to the mouth of the river—to Matamoras, Brownsville, Bagdad, and the coastal villages. Two of these were men with one idea: under cover of the disturbance and confusion of war, to slip down to the coast and get away with the gold.

One was the last actual survivor of the original six; the second was the son of the other survivor. The first, Duval, was an old man now. He found his way to Boca del Rio, where he sought out and secured a job as cook on Falcon Sackett's steamboat. Duval was a tough old man, and luckily for the men on the steamboat, an excellent cook.

Eric Stouten was twenty-four, a veteran of several years at sea, and a fisherman for some years before that. But when he found his way to Mexico it was as an enlistee in the cavalry assigned to the command of Captain Elam Kurbishaw.

Striking south on a foraging expedition, Captain Kurbishaw led his men into the village where once, long ago, the survivors from the treasure ship had come. That night, just before sundown, Trooper Stouten requested permission to speak to the commanding officer.

Captain Elam Kurbishaw was a tall, cool, desperate man. A competent field commander, he was also a man ready to listen to just such a proposal as Stouten had to offer.

Within the hour the commandant of the village was arrested, his quarters ransacked, and the old report of the interrogation of the prisoners found. With it was a single gold piece...kept as evidence that what was recorded there had, indeed, transpired.

The old commandant was dead. The report and the gold piece had been found when the present man took over. A long search had been carried on, covering miles of the coast. Nothing had been found.

The commandant was released; and as he walked away, Elam Kurbishaw, who left nothing to chance, turned and shot him.

A coldly meticulous man, Elam Kurbishaw was fiercely proud of his family, and its background, but well aware that the family fortune, after some years of mismanagement, was dwindling away. He and his two brothers were determined to renew those fortunes, and they had no scruples about how it was to be done.

Alone in his tent, he got out his map case and found a map of the shore line. Military activities concerned inland areas, and his map of the coast was not very detailed. But, studying the map, Kurbishaw was sure he could find the spot from the trooper's description. Laguna de Barril, he was sure, would be the place. But, as was the case of LaFitte's men, he placed the shipwreck too far north.

One other thing Kurbishaw did not know: his bullet had struck through the commandant, felling him, but not killing him. A tough man himself, he survived.

In the quiet of Jonas Locklear's study I heard the story unfold. How little, after all, had I known of my father! How much had even my mother known? That he had gone from the mountains I knew; how long I had never known. Now I learned he had sailed from Charleston in a square-rigger, had been an officer for a time on a river boat at Mobile, and then on the Rio Grande, when Taylor needed river men so desperately.

"Elam never had a chance to look," Jonas explained. "His command was shipped south to General Miles. The way I get it, the trooper remembered the offhand way Kurbishaw had shot the commandant, and again and again he saw Kurbishaw's ruthless way, and he began to regret telling him what he had, and that gave him the idea of deserting. But first he meant to kill Captain Kurbishaw, to let what Elam knew die with him."

After all, why did he need Kurbishaw? Eric Stouten was a good hand with a boat, a fine swimmer and diver, and the vessel lay in relatively shallow water.

The night before Chapultepec he took his knife and slipped into Kurbishaw's tent. He was lifting the knife when a voice stopped him. He turned his head, to see two Kurbishaws staring at him...another lay on the bed.

He cried out, lost his grip on his knife, and started to turn for the door, and the two men shot him.

"How do you know they didn't find the gold themselves?" I asked Locklear.

"They didn't know where to look. The Laguna de Barril is only one of many coves and inlets along that coast.

"The difficulty was, that young trooper had talked far too much. He had, among other things, told of the other man who was still around, the other pirate who had escaped...and who, he was sure, was now on one of the river boats on the Rio Grande.

"If they could not immediately find the gold, they would fix it so nobody else would, and they tried to murder old Duval. That brought your father into the fight, and his first run-in with the Kurbishaws. I don't know the circumstances, but when they tried to kill Duval, Falcon Sackett put a bullet into one of them, and then Duval told Falcon his story."

Bit by bit the story emerged, and bit by bit our own plans came into being. After that hot night in Jonas's cabin none of them ever gave up going back, and after my father disappeared, the Tinker hunted for him, and Jonas, too. Neither had any luck until Will Caffrey began to spend pa's gold, and Tinker followed the trail of that Spanish gold from Charleston to the mountains.

The Kurbishaws also traced the gold, and decided to kill me for fear I might go after it.

"Cortina has controlled that area off and on for years," Jonas said, "and many of his subordinates have been thieves or worse; however, nobody wants to see that much gold slipping through their fingers.

"After that talk in the cabin of my steamboat," he continued, "we waited until the time was right, and then slipped down there to look.

"The water in many places was shallow, there were many sand bars, and their location changed with each heavy blow. Twice we went aground, several times we were fired upon.

Then the war ended and we had no further excuse to be in the vicinity; and the local authorities, knowing something was hidden there, suspected everybody.

"Your father actually found the wreck and got away with some of the gold—got away, I might add, because he was uncommonly agile and gifted with nerve. And he tried to find us."

The Tinker glanced at me. "Had it been me I doubt I should have tried to find anybody, but it was Falcon Sackett, and he is a different man in every way."

Out of our talking a plan emerged. Jonas Locklear must, in any event, go to the ranch he owned on the Gulf coast. We would go with him, and then we would go to Mexico to buy cattle for a drive to Kansas, and to restock the ranch. This might call for several trips.

In this cattle-buying I should have to take first place, for either Jonas or the Tinker might be recognized, and to stay over a few hours south of the border would invite disaster.

Arrangements could be made by letter for me to pick up the herd, and then I would start north, holding them near the coast. Jonas and the Tinker would join me as cowhands, riding with other cowhands. When we had the herd close by where the treasure was believed to be, we would camp...and find our gold.

It was simple as that. Nobody, we believed, would suspect a cattleman of hunting for gold. It was a good cover, and we could find no flaws in it. There was water for cattle in brackish pools, there was good grass, so the route was logical.

"Are you sure," the Tinker asked me, "that your father left nothing to guide you to the ship? No map? No directions?"

"He gave me nothing when he left, and if there was a map he may have wanted it himself."

Jonas rose. "My brother-in-law may question you. You have been hired to work on my ranch, that is all."

"It is settled then?" the Tinker asked. "To Mexico?"

"How about it, Sackett?"

53

"Well," I said, "I never saw much gold, and always allowed as how I'd like to. This seems to be a likely chance." I shook hands with them.

"I only hope," I added, "that I'm half the man my father must have been."

FOUR

We fetched up to the ranch house shy of sundown. We'd been riding quite a spell of days, and while never much on riding, I had been doing a fair country job of it by the time we hauled rein in front of that soddy.

For that was what it was, a sod house and no more. Jonas Locklear had cut himself a cave out of a hillside and shored it up with squared timbers. Then he had built a sod house right up against it, built in some bunks, and there it was.

Only Locklear had been gone for some time, and when we fetched up in front of that soddy the door opened and a man came out.

He was no taller than me, but black-jawed and sour-looking. He wore a tied-down gun, and some folks would have decided from that he was a gunman. Me, I'd seen a few gunfighters, and they wore their guns every which way.

"I'm Locklear. I own this place. Who are you?"

The man just looked at him, and then as a second man emerged, the first one said, "Says he owns this place. Shall we tell it to him quick?"

"Might's well."

"All right." His eyes went from Locklear to the Tinker, and he said, "You don't own this place no more, Mr. Locklear. We do. We found it abandoned, we moved in. It's ours, we're givin' you until full dark to get off the place. The ranch stretches for ten miles thataway, so you'd best make a fast start."

Before Jonas could make reply, I broke in. Something about this man got in my craw and stuck there, and so I said, "You heard Jonas Locklear speak. This here ranch is deeded and proper, and not open to squatters. You gave us until full dark. Well, we ain't givin' you that much time. You got just two minutes to make a start."

His gun showed up. I declare, he got that thing out before I could so much as have it in mind.

"You draw fast," I said, "but you still got to shoot it, and before you kill me dead, I'll have lead in you. I'll shoot some holes in you, believe me. Now you take Cullen. When he was teaching me, he said—"

"Who? Who did you say?"

"Cullen"—I kept my face bland—"Cullen Baker. Now, when he was teaching me to draw, he said to—"

"Cullen Baker taught you to *draw?*" He looked around warily. "He ridin' with you?"

"He camps with us," I said. "What he does meanwhile I've no idea. Him an' Longley an' Lee, they traipse around the country a good deal. Davis police, they've been hustling Cullen some, so he said to me, 'South, that's the place. We'll go south.'"

This black-jawed man looked from me to the Tinker, and then he sort of backed up and said, "I'd no idea you was with Cullen Baker. I want no trouble with him, or any outfit he trails with."

"You've got a choice," I said, "Brownsville or Corpus Christi. When the rest of them get here, I figure to have coffee on. Cullen sets store by fresh black coffee."

They lit out, and after they had gone, the Tinker looked over at Jonas. "Did you ever see the like? Looks right down a gun barrel and talks them out of it."

"Cullen did camp with us," I said, "and there's no question that he liked our coffee."

Took us until midnight to clean that place out, but we did it. And then we turned in to sleep.

Sunup found us scouting around the range. Seemed like there was grass everywhere but no cattle, and then we did come on some cows and bulls in a draw, maybe twenty-five or thirty of them lazing in the morning sun. These were wild cattle. Owned cattle, mind you, but they'd run wild all their lives and were of no mind to be trifled with.

A longhorn is like nothing else you ever saw. If a man thinks he knows cattle, he should look over a longhorn first of all. The longhorn developed from cattle turned loose on the plains of Texas, growing up wild and caring for themselves; and for the country they were in, no finer or fiercer creature ever lived. There were some tough old mossy-horns in that outfit that would weigh sixteen hundred pounds or better, and when they held their heads up they were taller than our horses. They were mean as all get out, and ready to take after you if they caught you afoot. Believe me, a man needed a six-shooter and needed to get it into action fast if one of those big steers came for him.

Times had changed in Texas. When the Tinker and Locklear had been here before, cattle were worth about two dollars a head, and no takers, but now they were driving herds up the Shawnee Trail to the Kansas railheads and paying five and six dollars a head, selling them in Kansas at anywhere from eighteen to thirty dollars each. A trail drive was a money-making operation, if a man got through.

"Tinker," I said, "if we want to get rich in these western lands we should round up a few head and start for Kansas."

He grunted at me, that was all. Treasure was on his mind—bright, yellow gold with jewels and ivory and suchlike. I'll not claim it didn't set me to dreaming myself, but I am a practical man and there's nothing more practical than beef on the hoof when folks are begging for it on the fire.

We rode down into a little draw and there was a *jacal*, a Mexican hut. Around it was fenced garden space and a corral. As we rode up, I sighted a rifle barrel looking at us over a window sill, and the man who appeared in the doorway wore a belt gun. He was a tall, wiry Mexican, handsome but for a scar on his jaw. The instant his eyes touched Locklear he broke into a smile.

"Señor! Juana, the señor is back!"

The gun muzzle disappeared and a very pretty girl came to the door, shading her eyes at us.

"Tinker, Sackett...this is Miguel," Locklear said. "We are old friends."

They shook hands, and when Miguel offered his to me I took it and looked into the eyes of a man. I knew it would be good to have Miguel with us. There was pride and courage there, and something that told me that when trouble came, this man would stand.

This I respected, for of myself I was not sure. Every man wishes to believe that when trouble appears he will stand up to it, yet no man knows it indeed before it happens.

When trouble came at the river's crossing, I had faced up to it with the Tinker beside me, but it had happened too quickly for me to be frightened. And what if I had been alone?

Jonas and the Tinker were impressed by the bluff I worked on the man at the sod house, but I was not. To talk is easy, but what would I have done if he had fired? Would I indeed have been able to draw and return the fire?

My uncertainty was growing as I looked upon the fierce men about me, tough, experienced men who must many times have faced trouble. They knew themselves and what they would do, and I did not.

Would I stand when trouble came? Would I fight, or would I freeze and do nothing? I had heard tales of men who did just that, men spoken of with contempt, and these very tales helped to temper me against the time of danger.

Another thing was in my mind when I was lying ready for sleep, or was otherwise alone.

After the meeting with the man at the sod house I had known, deep down within me, that I would never be fast with a gun—at least, not fast enough. Despite all my practice, I had come to a point beyond which I could not seem to go.

This was something I could not and dared not speak of. But at night, or after we started the ride south for Matamoras, I tried to think it out.

Practice must continue, but now I must think always of just getting my gun level and getting off that first shot. That first shot must score, and I must shape my mind to accept the fact that I must fire looking into a blazing gun. I must return that fire even though I was hit.

South we rode, morning, noon, and night. South down the Shawnee Trail in moonlight and in sun, and all along the trail were herds of cattle—a few hundred, a few thousand, moving north for Kansas with their dust clouds to mark the way. We heard the prairie wind and the cowboy yells, and at night the prairie wolves that sang the moon out of the sky.

We smelled the smoke of the fires, endured the heat of the crowded bodies of the herd, and often of a night we stopped and yarned with the cowboys, sharing their fires and their food and exchanging fragments of news, or of stories heard.

There were freight teams, too. These were jerkline out-fits with their oxen or horses stretched out ahead of them hauling freight from Mexico or taking it back.

And there were free riders, plenty of them. Tough, hard-bitten men, armed and ready for trouble. Cow outfits return-ing home from Kansas, bands of unreconstructed renegades left over from the war, occasional cow thieves and robbers.

Believe me, riding in Texas had taught me there was more to the West than just wagon trains and cattle drives.

59

Folks were up to all sorts of things, legal and otherwise, and some of them forking the principle. That is, they sat astraddle of it, one foot on the legal side, the other on the illegal, and taking in money with both hands from both sides. Such business led to shooting sooner or later.

South we rode, toward the borderlands.

Our second day we overtook a fine coach and six elegant horses, with six outriders, tough men in sombreros, with Winchesters ready to use.

"Only one man would have such a carriage," Jonas said. "It will be Captain Richard King, owner of the ranch on Santa Gertrudis."

An outrider recognized Jonas and called out to him, and when King saw Jonas he had the carriage draw up. It was a hot, still morning and the trailing dust cloud slowly closed in and sifted fine red dust over us all.

"Jonas," King said, "my wife, Henrietta. Henrietta, this is Jonas Locklear."

Richard King was a square-shouldered, strongly built man with a determined face. It was a good face, the face of a man who had no doubts. I envied him.

"King was a steamboat captain on the Rio Grande," the Tinker explained to me in a low voice, "and after the Mexican War he bought land from Mexicans who now lived south of the border and could no longer ranch north of the line."

Later the Tinker told me more: how King had bought land from others who saw no value in grassland where Indians and outlaws roamed. One piece he bought was fifteen thousand acres, at two cents an acre.

Instead of squatting on land like most of them were doing, King had cleared title to every piece he bought. There was a lot of land to be had for cash, but you had to be ready to fight for anything you claimed, and not many wanted to chance it.

Brownsville was the place where we were to separate. At that time it was a town of maybe three thousand people, but busy as all get out. From here Miguel and I would go on alone.

Looking across toward Mexico, I asked myself what sort of fool thing I was getting into. Everybody who had anything to do with that gold had come to grief.

Nevertheless, I was going. Pa had a better claim to that gold than any man, and I aimed to have a try at it. And while I was going primed for trouble, I wasn't hunting it.

First off, I'd bought a new black suit and hat, as well as rougher clothes for riding. I picked out a pair of fringed shotgun chaps and a dark blue shirt. Then I bought shells for a new Henry rifle. The rifle itself cost me $43, and I bought a thousand rounds of .44's for $21. That same place I picked up a box of .36-caliber bullets for my pistol at $1.20 per hundred.

That Henry was a proud rifle. I mean it could really shoot. Men I'd swear by said it was accurate at one thousand yards, and I believed them. It carried eighteen bullets fully loaded.

My mare I'd left back at Miguel's place. Her time was close and she would need care. Miguel's woman was knowing thataway, so the mare was in good hands.

About noontime Miguel and me shook hands with the Tinker and Jonas, and then we crossed over the river and went into Matamoras.

My horse was a lineback dun, tough and trail wise. Miguel was riding a sorrel, and we led one pack horse, a bald-faced bay. We put up at a livery stable and I started up the street after arranging to meet Miguel at a *cantina* near the stable.

One thing I hadn't found to suit me was a good belt knife, and the Tinker wasn't about to part with one of his. I went into a store and started looking over some Bowie knives, and finally found one to please me—not that it was up to what the Tinker could do.

I paid for the knife, and then ran my belt through the

loop on the scabbard and hitched it into place. A moment there, I paused in the doorway. And that pause kept me from walking right into trouble.

Standing not ten feet away, on the edge of the boardwalk, was Duncan Caffrey!

He was facing away from me and I could see only the side of his face and his back, but I'd not soon forget that nose. I had fixed it the way it was.

No sooner had I looked at him than my eyes went to the man he spoke with, and I felt a little chill go down my spine. I was looking right into a pair of the blackest, meanest, cruelest eyes I ever did see.

The man wore a stovepipe hat and a black coat. His face was long, narrow, and deep-lined. He wore a dirty white shirt and a black tie that looked greasy, even at the distance.

Stepping outside, I walked slowly away in the opposite direction, my skin crawling because I felt they were looking at me. Yet when I reached the corner and looked back, they were still talking, paying me no mind.

Never before had I seen that man in the stovepipe hat, but I knew who he was.

The Bishop.

It had to be him. He had been described to me more than once, and he'd been mentioned by Caffrey that night when the Tinker and me listened from the brush.

Now, nobody needed to tell me that there's such a thing as accident, or coincidence, as some call it. I've had those things happen to me, time to time, but right at that moment I wouldn't buy that as a reason for Dun and the Bishop being in Matamoras. Whatever they were here for was connected with me. That much I was sure of and nothing would shake it.

Right there I had an idea of going back to Brownsville and telling the Tinker and Jonas. Trouble was, they'd think I was imagining things, or scaring out, or something like that.

What I did do was head for the *cantina* where I dropped

into a chair across the table from Miguel and said, "Enjoy that drink, because we're pulling out—tonight."

"*Tonight?*"

"Soon as ever we can make it without drawing eyes to us."

Sitting there at the table, I drank a glass of beer and told him why. Even down here they had heard of the Bishop, so Miguel was ready enough.

"One thing," he said, "we must ride with great care, for there was word that a prisoner escaped from prison and is at large to the south of here. They believe he will come to the border, and the soldiers search for him."

It was past midnight when we walked through the circle of lemon light under the livery-stable lantern. The hostler sat asleep against the wall, his *serape* about his shoulders. Music tinkled from the *cantina*...there was a smell of hay, and of fresh manure, of leather harness, and of horses.

As we walked our horses from the stable I leaned over and dropped a *peso* in the lap of the hostler.

Riding past the *cantina*, I glanced back. I thought I saw, in a dark doorway next to the *cantina*, the boot-toes and the tip of a hat belonging to a very tall man. I could have been mistaken.

We rode swiftly from the town. The night was quiet except for the insects that sang in the brush. A long ride lay before us. The cattle about which we had inquired were at a ranch southwest of Santa Teresa...the gold lay somewhere off the coast we would parallel.

So far as we knew, pa was the only man who knew exactly where that sunken ship lay. The Kurbishaws had killed the man who told them of it, thinking they could find it from the description. Captain Elam Kurbishaw's only map that showed the coast was vague, and had indicated only one inlet on that stretch of coast, where actually there were several. More to the point, there was a long stretch of coast that lay behind an outlying sand bar. If the ship had succeeded in getting through one of the openings in the shore line, it would be lost in a maze of inlets, channels, and bays. Looking for it would be like looking for one cow that bawled in a herd of five thousand.

"Soldiers may stop us," Miguel warned. "It is well to give them no displeasure, for the soldiers can be worse than *bandidos*."

As we rode along, my mind kept thinking back to Gin Locklear and that snippy little Marsha.

Marsha was fourteen...she'd be up to marrying in maybe two years, and I pitied the man who got her. As for Gin, she was older than me, but she was a woman to take a man's eye, and to talk a man's tongue, too. It was no wonder Jonas set such store by her.

It lacked only a little of daybreak when we turned off the trail into the brush. We went maybe half a mile off the traveled way before we found a hollow where there was grass and a trickle of water. We staked out the horses and bedded down for sleep. Miguel took no time about it, but sleep was long in coming to me.

Thoughts kept going round in my mind, and pa was in the middle of them. I thought how pa was always teaching me things. Had he maybe taught me where that gold was, and me not knowing?

And then my mind was sorting out memories and feeling the sadness they brought.

Ma was gone....Pa? Who could ever know about pa? Those were bad days for travelers and folks who went a-yondering. Chances were the Bald Knobbers had got him...or somebody from ambush.

I'd never believe it was them Kurbishaws.

FIVE

We saw no more of the Bishop or the Kurbishaws on the trail in the next few days.

We found Santa Teresa a sleepy, pleasant Mexican village, with hens scratching in the street, and the best *tortillas* I'd eaten up to then, or for a long time after.

The *hacienda* where I bargained for and bought three hundred head of cattle was another pleasant place, and when we started the cattle back toward the border they loaned me three *vaqueros* to help until my own hands joined us—they were to meet us in camp just north of Santa Teresa.

The range from which we bought our cattle had been overstocked and the cattle were thin, but they showed an immediate liking for the grass of the coastland and its plentiful salt. We were four days driving from the *hacienda* to the camp north of Santa Teresa, but when we reached the camp there was no one there.

Here the *vaqueros* were to leave us, and here we must hold our stock until help came from the north. Five men could handle three hundred head without too much trouble when they were intent upon stuffing their lean bellies with good grass, but from there on it would be more difficult.

Scarcely were we camped, with a fire going, when we heard a rush of horses and suddenly our camp was surrounded by soldiers, their rifles leveled on us.

Their officer was a lean and savage man. He rode around the herd, inspecting the brands, then he wheeled up to the fire.

"Who is in charge here?" he asked in Spanish.

Miguel gestured to me. "The Americano. We have bought the cattle from Señor Ulloa. We drive them to Texas."

"You are lying!"

"No, señor," one of the *vaqueros* spoke up quickly. "I am of the *hacienda* of Ulloa. Three of us have ridden with the cattle to this point. Here their own riders join them. It is of a truth, señor."

The officer looked at me, his eyes cold and unfriendly. "Your name?"

"Orlando, señor." It seemed possible he might have heard the name Sackett, although it would have been long ago.

He studied me without pleasure. "Do you know Señor King?"

"We spoke with him two days ago. He was driving to Brownsville with the señora."

King was well thought of on both sides of the border, and to know him seemed the wise thing.

He considered the situation a bit, then said: "One thing, señor. A prisoner has escaped. We want him. If you should come upon him, seize him at once and send a rider for me. Anyone rendering assistance to him will be shot." Without further words, he wheeled his horse.

When they had ridden away, the *vaquero* turned to me, his expression grave. "Señor, that was Antonio Herrara—a very bad man. Avoid him if you can."

They were packing to leave, and seemed more than anxious to get away, and I couldn't find it in my heart to go a-blaming them. Surely, this was no trouble of theirs.

After they had gone there was nothing we could do but ride herd on our cattle, and wait.

Sometimes a man is a fool, and I had a feeling that when I left my mare to go traipsing after gold money I'd been more of a fool than most. I'd sure enough be lying if I said I wasn't scared, for that Herrara shaped up like a mean man, and we were in his country where he was the law.

Miguel took the first ride around, bunching the cattle for night. They seemed willing enough to rest, being chock full of good grass like they were. Me, I kept looking up trail toward the border and a-hoping for those riders.

What if Jonas and the Tinker couldn't make it? What if Herrara spotted them as escaped prisoners themselves?

"Miguel," I said, when he stopped by on his circling, "come daybreak we're pushing on, riders or no riders. We're going to head for the border."

He nodded seriously. "It is wise, *amigo*. That Herrara, he is a bad man."

The place where we were was a meadow four, five miles out of Santa Teresa and on an arm of the sea. There was brush around, and some marshy land.

"That prisoner," Miguel said, "he will not be taken easily. He killed a guard in escaping, and he has been much tortured. It is said, señor"—Miguel paused expressively—"that he was believed to know something of a treasure."

"A treasure?" I asked mildly.

"Si, señor. It is a treasure much talked of, a treasure of the pirate, LaFitte. For thirty years and more men have sought it along the shore to the north. Most of all, Antonio Herrara and his father, the commandant of this area."

What could a man say to that? Only it made me itch all the more to get that herd moving.

"Miguel, an hour before daylight we will start the herd. Twenty miles tomorrow."

"It is a long drive, señor," he said doubtfully.

"Twenty miles—no less."

When the moon lifted, the cattle rose to stretch their legs and move around. Far off, there was a sound of coyotes, and closer by we could hear the rustle of the surf. The waters of the Laguna Madre were close by, the sea itself lay out beyond the bar, at least twenty-five miles away.

Miguel came in and, after coffee, turned in. Mounting the dun, I circled the cattle, singing softly to let them know that they were not alone, and that the shadow they saw moving was me. Nevertheless, there was a restlessness in them I could not explain, but I put it down to my ignorance of cattle.

With the first gray of dawn I stopped by to wake up Miguel.

He sat up and put on his hat, then pulled on his boots. He reached for the big, fire-blackened coffee pot, and shook it in surprise. "You drink much coffee, señor."

"One cup," I said. "I was afraid to stop for more. Something was bothering the cattle."

He emptied out the pot into his cup. "There were at least five cups in this, *amigo*. No less, certainly. I made the coffee myself, and know what we drank. It is a pot for ten men."

"Pack up," I said, "let's move 'em."

They seemed willing enough to go, and an old blue-roan steer moved out and took the lead, as he had done all the way from the *hacienda*.

As they moved, they fed; and we let them for the first two or three hours. Then we stepped up the speed a bit, because both of us wanted distance between us and last night's camp.

Most of the time I rode with a hand ready to grab a gun. From time to time I reached for that Walch Navy, and the butt had a mighty friendly feeling. Nothing feels better when trouble shapes than the butt of a good pistol.

We kept scanning the trail ahead, hoping for a sign of

our riders. Lucky for us the cattle seemed to want to get away from that place as much as we did.

There were no trees. Meadows of grass appeared here and there, and sometimes there'd be grass for miles, but between the trail and the sea there was a regular forest of brush. Here and there were signs that the sea had on occasion even come this far. The last time must have been the great hurricane of 1844. If there had been another of such power since, we hadn't heard of it, but the one of '44 was well known.

The cattle drifted steadily. The heat rising from their bunched bodies was as stifling as the dust. Only once in a while did one of the steers cut loose and try to stray from the column. But for two riders it was too many cattle, and our horses would soon be worn to nothing.

Off to the right was the sea...that was east. As far as we were from it, I turned again and again to look that way, for though we had been close a time or two, I had never yet seen the ocean. It gave a man an odd feeling to know all the miles upon miles of water that lay off there.

Somewhere out there, lying on the bottom close in to shore, was a ship loaded with gold and silver, with gems maybe, and suchlike. Pa had found it and brought gold from it, and pa must have come back again after he left me. It would be like him to let on he was going for fur, then to trail south where the gold was. Why trap for skins, when the price of thousands of them lay off that coast in shallow water?

It set a man to sweating, just to think of that much gold. It had never really got to me until now. And after all, that was what we'd come for. We hadn't really come for a few hundred scrawny Mexican steers....I wondered how long it would take that Herrara to figure that out.

Not that a few folks weren't buying Mexican stock. With the prices offered in the railhead towns, it was a caution what folks would do to lay hands on a few steers.

But this gold, now. LaFitte, he wasn't only a pirate and slave trader, he was a blacksmith in New Orleans with a shop where slaves did the work, and he and his brother...now how did I know that?

Had the Tinker mentioned it? Or Jonas? Jonas, probably, when we were talking. Yet the notion stayed with me that I'd heard it before.

Now I was imagining things. I couldn't call to mind any mention of Jean LaFitte—not before we came up to that plantation house after leaving San Augustine. Not before we met Jonas.

The dun was streaked with sweat and I could tell by the way he moved that he was all in. We hadn't come twenty miles, either. Not by a long shot.

Miguel dropped back beside me, and that horse of his looked worse than mine.

"Señor," he said, "we must stop."

"All right," I said, "but not for the night. We'll take ourselves a rest and then push on."

He looked at me, then shrugged. I knew what he was thinking. If we kept on like this we'd be driving those cattle afoot. We should have a remuda, and Jonas was supposed to be bringing one south. We weren't supposed to drive these cattle not even a foot after the *vaqueros* left us.

We turned the herd into a circle and stopped them where the grass was long and a trickle of water made a slow way, winding across the flatland toward the dunes that marked the lagoon's edge.

We found a few sticks and nursed a fire into boiling water for coffee. Miguel hadn't anything to say. Like me, he was dead beat. But I noticed something: like me, he had wiped his guns free of dust and checked the working mechanism.

"I ain't going to no prison," I said suddenly. "I just ain't a-honing for no cell. That there Herrara wants me, he's got to get me the hard way."

"We have no chance," Miguel said.

"You call it then," I said. "Do we fight?"

"We try to run. We try to dodge. When we can no longer do either, we shoot." He grinned at me, and suddenly the coffee tasted better.

I don't know why I was so much on the shoot all to once, but lately I'd heard so many stories of what happened in those prisons that I just figured dying all to once would be better. Besides, I didn't like that Herrara, and I might get him in my sights. Why, a man who could bark a squirrel could let wind through his skull. That's what I told myself.

Besides, I hadn't shot that Henry .44 at anything. Nor the Walch Navy, as far as that went.

We lay by the trail for three, four hours. We rubbed our horses down good, we led them to water, we let them eat that good grass. And afterwards we saddled again, and mounted up.

The steers were against it. They'd had enough for the day, and were showing no sign of wanting to go further. We cut this one and that one a slap with our *riatas*, and finally they lined out for Texas.

You don't take a herd nowhere in a hurry. Not unless they take a notion to stampede. Maybe eight to ten miles is a good day, with a few running longer than that. We'd been dusting along since four o'clock in the morning and it was past four in the evening now. When they first started, they fed along the way, so we'd made slow time. All I wanted was a little more distance. If we could get where I wanted to hold up, we'd be about twenty-five miles or so from the border.

If a difficulty developed, I figured I could run that far afoot with enough folks a-shooting after me. Anyway, I'd be ready to give it a try. I kept in mind that I'd no particular want to see the inside of one of Mr. Herrara's jail cells.

I was a lover, not a fighter. That's what I said to myself, though I'd no call to claim either. I was only judging where my interests lay.

My thoughts went to Gin Locklear—what a woman! I'd blame no man setting his cap for her, although the way I figured, it would take some standup sort of man to lay a rope on her.

That Marsha now...she was only a youngster, and a snippy one, but if she went on the way she'd started she might take after Gin...and I could think of nothing in woman's clothes it would be better for a girl to take after.

Shy of midnight we held up near salt water, with high brush growing around, and not more than four miles or so off was the tiny village of Guadalupe. Right close was a long arm of the Gulf.

"We will camp here," I said. "There is fresh water from a spring near the knoll over there."

Miguel looked at me strangely. "How does it happen that you know this?" he asked. "Señor Locklear said you had never been to Mexico."

"I—" I started to answer him, to say I know not what, perhaps to deny that I had been here or knew anything about it. Yet I did know.

Or did I? Supposing there was no spring there? How much had Locklear said?

The spring was there, and Locklear had said nothing about it. I knew that when I looked at the spring, for there, in a huge old timber that was down, there were initials carved. And carved in a way I'd seen only once before, that being in the mountains of Tennessee.

FSct

Just like that...carved there plain as day, like pa had carved them on that old pine near the house.

He had been here, all right. Miguel did not notice the initials, or if he did he paid them no mind. I doubt if he would have connected them with Falcon Sackett, and I was not sure how much had been told him. Something, of course...but not all.

Believe me, those steers were ready to bed down. We bunched them close for easy holding, and they scarcely took time to crop a bait of grass before they tucked their legs under them and went to chewing cud and sleeping.

Miguel wasn't much behind them. "Turn in," I said, "and catch yourself some shut-eye. I'll stand watch."

It wasn't in him to argue, he was that worn-out. Me, I was perked up, and I knew why. Pa had told me of this place, and I'd forgotten. Yet it had been lying back there in memory, and probably I'd been driving right for this place without giving it thought.

Now the necessary thing was to recollect just what it was pa had told me. He surely wouldn't tell me the part of it without he told me all.

When had he told me? Well, that went back a mite. Had to be before I was ten, the way I figured. He rode off when I was eleven and ma had been sick for some time before that, and he was doing mighty little talking to me aside from what was right up necessary.

It wasn't as if he'd told me one or two stories. He was forever yarning to me, and probably when he told me this one he'd stressed detail, he'd told it over and over again to make me remember. Somehow I was sure of that now.

Maybe I'd been plain tired out by the story. Maybe it hadn't seemed to have much point, but the fact was that he must have told me where the treasure was, and all I had to do was let my memory take me there.

Thing was, suppose it didn't come to me right off? I'd have to stay, and I'd need explanation for that. The fast drive we'd made would help. I could let on I didn't know much about cattle; and if anybody who talked cows to me did so more than a few minutes, they'd know I didn't know anything about them.

So I'd let on like I'd driven the legs off the cattle, to say nothing of our horses, and we were laying up alongside this water to recuperate.

That much decided, the next thing was to get my memory to operating. But the difficulty with a memory is that it doesn't always operate the way a body wants. Seems contrary as all get out, and when you want to remember a particular thing, that idea is shunted off to one side.

Rousting around, I got some sticks, some dead brush, and a few pieces of driftwood left from storms, and I made a fire. Then I put water on for coffee.

All of a sudden I felt my skin prickle, and I looked over at the dun. Tired as he was, he had his head up and his ears pricked. His nostrils were spreading and narrowing as he tried the air to see what it was out there.

That old Walch Navy was right there in my belt, and I eased it out a mite so's it was ready to hand.

Something was out there.

Me, I never was one to believe in ha'nts. Not very much, that is. Fact is, I never believed in them at all, only passing a graveyard like—well, I always walked pretty fast and felt like something was closing in on me.

No, I don't believe in ha'nts, but this here was a coast where dead men lay. Why, the crew of the gold ship must have been forty, fifty men, and all of them dead and gone.

Something was sure enough out there. That lineback dun knew it and I knew it. Trouble was, he had the best idea of what it was, and he wasn't talking. He was just scenting the air and trying to figure out for sure. Whatever it was, he didn't like it—I could tell that much. And I didn't either.

I felt like reaching over and shaking Miguel awake, only he'd think I was spooked. And you know something? I was.

This here was country where folks didn't come of a night, if at any time. It was a wild, lonely place, and there was nothing to call them.

I taken out that Walch Navy and, gripping it solid, I held it right there in my lap with the firelight shining on it. And you can just bet I felt better.

Out there beyond the fire I suddenly heard the sand *scrooch*. You know how sand goes underfoot sometimes. Kind of a crunch, yet not quite that. Heard it plain as day, and I lifted that .36 and waited.

Quite a spell passed by, and all of a sudden the dun, who'd gone back to feeding, upped with his head again. Only this time he was looking off toward the trail from the north, and he was all perked up like something interesting was coming. Not like before.

He had his ears up and all of a sudden he whinnied— and sure enough, from out of the darkness there came another whinny. And then I heard the sound of a horse coming, and Miguel, he sat up.

We both stayed there listening and, like fools, neither of us had sense enough to get back out of the firelight—like the Tinker had done that night when Baker, Lee, and Longley paid us the visit…and a few dozen other times along the trail.

We both just sat there and let whoever it was ride right up to the fire.

And when that slim-legged, long-bodied horse came into the firelight and I saw who it was, I couldn't believe it. Nor could Miguel. If we'd seen the ghost I'd been expecting, we wouldn't have been more surprised.

It was Gin Locklear.

SIX

S he rode side-saddle, of course, her skirt draped in graceful folds along the side of the horse, her gloved hand holding the bridle reins just as if she hadn't ridden miles through bandit-infested country to get here. She was just as lovely as when I last saw her.

She taken my breath. Coming up on us out of the night so unexpected-like, and after all the goings-on outside of camp...I hadn't a thought in my head, I was that rattled.

It came on me that I'd best help her from the saddle and I crossed over and took her hand, but it was not until she was actually on the ground that I saw the dark shadows under her eyes and the weariness in her face.

"Miguel," I said, "you handle the horse. I'll shake up some fresh coffee."

I dumped the pot and rinsed it, and put in fresh water from the spring. Then I stirred up the fire.

"I had to shoot a man," Gin said suddenly.

Those big eyes of hers handed me a jolt when I looked into them. "Did you kill him?"

"I don't think so."

Miguel turned toward us. "It would have been better had he been killed. Now he will speak of a beautiful señorita riding alone to the south, and others will come."

"There were two men with him," she said, "but this one held my bridle when they ordered me from the saddle. They were shouting and drinking and telling me what they were going to do.

"Of course, they did not see my gun and did not expect me to shoot, but I did shoot the man holding the horse, and then I got away. One of them had hold of my saddle and he tried to grab me. He fell, I think."

"Where was this?"

"Outside of Matamoras. Only a few miles out."

Then she said, "I came to help. Jonas and the Tinker have been arrested—Jonas, at least. He was recognized."

"Recognized? By whom?"

"They came looking for him, just as if they knew he would be there."

My first thought was of Franklyn Deckrow. He was the one with the most to gain if Jonas was not permitted to return. Of course, he might have been seen by someone who remembered him from prison.

It was little enough I knew of the Deckrow deal, but from all I'd gathered Deckrow had run the plantation into debt and Jonas believed it had been done deliberately so Deckrow could later buy up the mortgages and gain possession. If so, he could have sent a rider on a fast horse to Matamoras.

"You shouldn't have come," I said. "This is no place for a woman."

"The place for a woman," she said, smiling at me, "is where she is needed. I ride as well as most men, and I have a fine horse. Also, I've lived on a ranch most of my life."

"Did you see anybody as you came along the trail?"

She looked at me curiously. "Not for miles. I've never

seen a more deserted road, and if I hadn't seen a reflection of your campfire I might have gone right on by."

"You didn't circle the camp?"

"No."

Miguel was looking at me now, and I noticed he had his rifle in hand.

"There was somebody around the camp. Somebody or some *thing*."

Miguel stared uneasily at the blackness beyond the fire. Neither of us liked to think there was somebody or something out there whom we could not see.

"Maybe we should go, señor?"

"No, we'll sit right here and let the stock rest up." That was my plan, but the arrival of Gin had put a crimp in it. If outlaws were going to come hunting her, we'd be in trouble a-plenty.

"Come daybreak," I said, "we'll move the herd."

"Where, señor?"

"Yonder, I think we can find a place to hold the cattle. Maybe some of the other men will get through. That Tinker— he's a sly one. If he had any warning, no law is going to latch onto him."

Gin made herself comfortable on my bed. I stirred up the fire and finished off what coffee the three of us hadn't drank, and ate a couple of cold *tortillas*.

At daybreak the wind was off the sea, and you could feel the freshness of it, with a taste like no other wind.

Wide awake, I thought of those initials of pa's. Pa had left that sign, and he'd left it for himself, or mayhap for me. He was a planning man, pa was, and one likely to foresee.... I think he taken time deliberately to teach me where that gold was. The trouble was, I'd gone ahead and forgotten.

Some things I did remember. He'd taught me to mark a trail, Indian fashion. Now, suppose he had marked this one? If he had, he would have added his own particular ways to it, but meanwhile, I planned to look around. If I found no sign I was going to drive that herd where I felt it should go, with no scouting for grass, or anything. Maybe out of my hidden thoughts would come the memory of what pa had taught me, to guide our way.

I taken a circle around camp, and I found no sign—nothing left by pa that I could make out.

That isn't to say I didn't find sign of another kind, and when I seen that track I felt a chill go right up my spine that stood every hair on end.

What I found were wolf tracks, but wolf tracks bigger than any wolf that ever walked—any *normal* sort of wolf, that is. These wolf tracks were big as dinner plates.

Well, I stopped right there, looking down at those tracks, and the other two came over to look. Miguel's face turned white when he saw the tracks, and even Gin kind of caught at my arm.

We had both heard tell of werewolves, and certainly Miguel knew the stories about them.

Me, I was thinking of something else. I was thinking of where those tracks were. Soon I scouted around, and a far piece away, like whatever it was had been taking giant strides, I found another track, this one set deep in the sod.

The tracks circled about the water hole at the spring. Whatever it was, it was trying to get to water, but the water had been lighted by our fire, with one of us setting awake.

All of a sudden I saw something that made me forget all about werewolves and ha'nts and such. Far as that goes, I'd never heard tell of a thirsty ghost.

What I saw was something back in the brush, and at first it didn't look like much of a find, except that there was no reason for it being where it was. It was a broken reed, and it lay right on the edge of a bunch of mesquite.

Taking up the reed, I drew it out, and you know, there were several pieces of reed stuck one into another until they were all of eight or nine feet long. Stretched out, they reached from the spring's pool to the brush nearby.

"What is it?" Gin asked.

"Somebody wanted a drink, and wanted it bad, so he made a tube of these reeds, breaking them off to be rid of the joints and putting them together so he could suck water through them. He must have siphoned water right out of the pool into his mouth while I was just a-setting there."

Nobody said anything, and I nosed around a mite, studying the brush, and finally finding where the man or whatever it was had knelt.

There, too, I found the wolf tracks.

"Two-legged wolf," I said, "wearing some kind of coarse-woven jeans or pants. See here?" I showed them the place in the brush. "That's where he knelt whilst siphoning the water."

Following the tracks back from the brush, I said, "He's big—look at the length of that stride. I can't match it without running."

I studied the reed tube again. "Canny," I said. "Like something the Tinker might do."

"We should go," Gin suggested.

"No," I said, "not without what we came after. We have come too far and risked too much."

"But how can you hope to find it?" Gin said. "You've no idea where to look."

"Maybe I have. Maybe I am just beginning to recollect some things pa told me."

The wind was blowing harder and the sky was gray and overcast. The cattle wandered to the water in small groups, then returned to the bedding ground to graze or rest. They showed no restlessness, and seemed content to hold to the low spots out of the wind.

I cut some sod with a machete, and made a wall to protect our fire from the wind, adding just enough fuel to keep some coals. Miguel was worried, which I could see plain enough, and so was Gin.

Meanwhile I was doing some figuring. Jonas was in prison, and the Tinker might well be, so that left whatever was to be done up to me. Gin was with us, which she hadn't ought to be, the country being torn up with trouble the way it was, and somewhere close by was that ship filled with gold.

Jonas needed his share to get his mortgage paid off, and the Tinker wanted his. As far as that goes, I wasn't going to buck or kick if somebody handed me some of that there gold.

Around the fire at breakfast, Miguel told me a mite about Herrara. He was a lieutenant of General Juan Nepomuceno Cortina, usually called Cheno, and part of the time he was a soldier with a legitimate rank, and part of the time an outlaw, depending on who was in power in Mexico and on his own disposition at the moment.

Of good family, Cortina had become a renegade, but one with a lot of followers. He was a shrewd fighter, risking battle only when it suited him, and running when it didn't. He was a man of uncertain temperament, but dangerous enough and strong enough to handle the pack of wolves that followed him.

Frequently, they raided across the border into Texas and had run off thousands of head of Texas cattle. Yet he had good men following him, too, and on occasion he could be both gallant and generous. But generally speaking, he was a man to fight shy of.

As for Herrara, he was one of the wolves, fierce as an Apache, and by all accounts treacherous.

Leaving Miguel by the fire, with his horse saddled, to keep an eye on the cows, Gin and I rode off through the brush, hunting the water's edge.

We hadn't far to go. A long gray finger of water came twisting through the grass, leading some distance away to a larger body of water like a bay. There we could see the white, bare bones of an ancient boat, much too small for what we were looking for... which, anyway, was by all accounts down underwater.

My Henry was in the saddle boot, and Gin carried one also. But what I kept ready to hand was that Walch Navy. I liked the feel of that gun.

As we rode we saw nothing—only a low shore of gray-green grass, the gray water looking like a sheet of steel, the reeds bending under the wind, gulls wheeling and crying overhead. Whitecaps were showing on the water.

It might have been a world never seen by man. No tracks, no ashes of old fires, nothing man had built but the stark white ribs of that old boat.

"It's cold," Gin said.

Her face looked pinched, and the place was depressing her, as it was me.

Yet, wild and lonely as it was, the country had an eerie sort of charm like nowhere I'd ever seen. Toward the Gulf I could see the dunes of sand heaped by wind and wave, and somewhere out there was a long bar that stretched miles away to the south.

A barren desolate land. In spite of this, the place seemed to be working a charm on me.

"Let's go back," Gin said.

We turned and made our start, riding along the shore. The wind was blowing stronger, the brush and reeds bending before it. A few cold, spitting drops of rain began to fall.

The place to which we had driven the herd was in a cul-de-sac, with the sea on three sides—long arms of the sea where the water had flowed in over low ground or the working of the waves had hollowed it out.

To the east was a long, snake-like arm of the sea that nowhere was over a quarter of a mile wide. South and southwest the coves were wider.

The grass was good, and the cattle were protected by thick brush from the worst of the wind. Most of these cattle had at one time or another grazed along the shore, and like Shanghai Pierce and his "sea lions," as he called the longhorns that swam back and forth from the coast to Padre Island, they were used to the sea and were good swimmers.

"I like it," I said suddenly, gesturing toward the country around us. "It's almighty wild and lonely, but I take to it."

83

We drew up and looked back. The sweep of the shore had an oddly familiar look to it that started excitement in me. I frowned and tried to remember, but nothing came.

"Pa must have told me about this place," I said. "I can feel it. This here's where the gold is, somewhere about here."

"Your father must have been an interesting man."

So, a-setting there in the chill wind, I talked about him as I recalled him, big, powerful and dark, straight and tall. An easy-moving man who never seemed in a hurry, and yet could move swift as any striking snake when need be.

"He'd never let be," I said, "not with him knowing where that gold is. He'd come back for it. Ma never wanted him to go back.

"You see, before pa and ma met, he had trouble with her brothers, the Kurbishaws, and over this gold. There were three of them, led by Captain Elam. The other two were Gideon and Eli.

"I never got the straight of it, although from time to time I'd hear talk around the house, but they were after the gold the same time pa was, and they tried to run him off. Pa never was much on running, as I gather.

"Later on, with some of this gold in his jeans, he went to Charleston and cut quite a swath about town. And there he met ma. They taken to each other, and it wasn't until she invited him home that he met her brothers face to face and knew who they were."

"It sounds very dramatic."

"Must have been, pa being what he was and those Kurbishaws hating him like they did. I knew little about it, but I gathered more from talking with the Tinker and Jonas ...that helped me to piece together things I'd heard as a child."

We walked our horses on, the dun's mane blown by the wind. It gave me an odd feeling to know that pa had more than likely watched and walked this same shore, maybe many times, a-hunting that gold.

Odd thing, I'd never thought of my pa as a person. I

expect a child rarely does think of his parents that way. They are a father and a mother, but a body rarely thinks of them as having hopes, dreams, ambitions and desires and loves. Yet day by day pa was now becoming more real to me than he had ever been, and I got to wondering if he ever doubted himself like I did, if he ever felt short of what he wished to be, if he ever longed for things beyond him that he couldn't quite put into words.

"You'd like pa," I said suddenly. "The more I think of him the more I like him, myself. I mean other than just as a father. I figure he's the kind of man I'd like to ride the trail with, and I guess that's about as much as a man can say."

Ahead of us I saw a mite of grass bunched up, and I drew rein sudden and felt my breath tight in my throat. Gin started on, but when she saw my face she stopped.

"Orlando, *what is it?*"

It was a small tuft of grass kind of bunched up, and some other grass stems had been used to tie a knot around the top of the bunch.

There it sat, kind of out of the way and accidental-like, but it was no accident. Maybe many men used that trail marker—no doubt Indians did. But I knew one man who'd used it, and who knew I'd spot such a thing.

My pa.

"Gin"—I couldn't speak above a whisper—"pa's been here."

She looked at me, her eyebrows raised a little. "Of course, when he found the gold."

"No...recent. Maybe the past two or three days."

Swinging down, I slid an arm through the loop of the bridle reins and squatted down to look closer. That marker had been made within the past couple of days, for the broken grass used to tie around the bunch was still green.

Straightening up, I looked all around, taking my time. Whoever had made that marker intended for it to be seen, but not by just anybody. Nobody would see it unless he was trained to look for sign.

It stood all by itself, though. I mean, there was grass all around and some brush, but no other markers. That meant that what it was intended to mark was close by, within the range of my eyes. It was up to me to see it. Yet, looking all around, I saw nothing. The clouded sky, the gray, white-capped water, the green grass growing just short of knee-high, the scattered brush, the reeds along the shore...

The reeds!

Reaching up, I taken my Henry from the boot. "You stand watch, Gin. Watch everything, not just me."

For two, three minutes I didn't move. I stood there beside my horse and I studied those reeds, and I studied them section by section, taking a piece maybe ten foot square and studying it careful, then moving on to another square.

Trailing the bridle reins, I stepped away from the horse and worked my way carefully through the reeds. What I had spotted was an open space among the reeds, which might mean an inlet of water, for there were several such around. However, when I got to that open place—minding myself to break no reeds and to move with care—I found a low hive, a mound-like hut of reeds made by drawing the tops together and tying them, then weaving other reeds through the rooted ones. It was maybe eight feet long by four or five wide.

Room enough for a man to sleep.

"I'm friendly," I said, speaking low but so I could be heard. "I'm hunting no trouble."

There was no answer.

Easing forward a bit, I spotted the opening that led inside, and kneeling, I eased forward. I spoke once more, and there was no response. Then I stuck my head inside.

The hut was empty.

The ground inside must have been damp, so close to the water, and it had been covered by several hastily woven mats of reeds, with grass thrown atop of them.

I backed out and stood up.

My father had taught me to build an emergency shelter

just thataway from reeds, cane, or slim young trees. He taught me when I was six years old, and I'd not forgotten.

Pa was here.

I was sure of it now. That marker, just the way he used to use them, something to call attention, not necessarily to indicate a trail…and now this.

When I got back to the horse I put a foot in the stirrup and swung my leg over the saddle. Gin was waiting for me to tell her, and I did.

"Pa's close by," I said. "I've got an idea that prisoner Herrara is hunting is my father."

"You're sure he's near?"

So I told her what I had seen, and explained a bit about it.

If he was close by, he would find me—unless he was lying hurt.

Even so, he would find me or let me know some way, so I turned and we started back to the herd. We rode more swiftly now, eager to get back.

There was so much inside me I wasn't looking out as sharp as I should have. We came riding around the brush, and there were fifteen or twenty riders, and down in the middle of them was Miguel.

Miguel was on the ground, and his face was all blood. A thick-set Mexican was standing over him with a quirt in his hand. Herrara sat his horse nearby.

Only thing saved me was they'd been so busy they weren't listening, and a horse on soft sod doesn't make a whole lot of disturbance.

Lucky for me I was carrying that Henry out in the open. She swung up slick as a catfish on a mudbank and I eared back the hammer.

They all heard *that*.

Their heads came around like they were all on string, but the one I had covered was Herrara himself.

"Call that man off," I said, "or I'll kill you."

He looked at me, those black eyes flat and steady as a rattler's. I'll give him this. There was no yellow showing. He looked right into that rifle barrel and he said, "You shoot me, señor, and you are dead in the next instant."

Me, I wasn't being bluffed. Not that day. I looked right along that barrel and I said, "Then I'll be the second man to die. When I fall, you'll lie there to make me a cushion."

We looked at each other, and he read me right. Whatever happened, I'd kill.

"And the lady? What happens to her if we die?"

"We'd never know about that, would we?" I said. "I think she'd take care of herself, however, and if anything happened to her, I don't think Cheno would like it."

"What do you know of Cheno?"

"Me? Next to nothing, but the señorita's family were good friends to Cheno's family when he lived north of the border. How else would a mere woman have the courage to ride alone into Mexico?"

He was listening, and I think he believed me. Sure I was lying. Maybe her family had known the Cortina family, and maybe they never had. But I was talking to save the lady trouble, and maybe some talk for my own skin as well.

He did not like it, because it tied his hands, and he wasn't letting up yet.

"Why do you stop *here?*"

"Hell," I said offhand, "you're a better cowman than I am. I ran the legs off those steers getting them up here. I got a girl north of the border, and I wanted to get back. Those other hands never showed, so we pushed 'em hard and nearly killed our horses. We had to rest."

It was true, of course, and I made plenty of sense, and that was one thing I had planned just that way. I wanted that story to tell if he came up on us again.

"Has anyone come to your camp other than the señorita?" he asked then.

"If they did, I didn't see them. We've been hoping somebody would come by who had some *frijoles* to sell. We're short on grub."

He asked a few more questions, and then they rode off, but I'd a hunch they would leave somebody to watch, or maybe none of them would go very far.

Miguel's face was cut and swollen. He had been lashed several times across the face and struck once with the butt because he could tell them nothing.

Now he washed the blood from his face and then looked around at me. "Careful, *amigo*. That one will kill you now, or you shall kill him. You faced him over a gun and made him back up."

"Twenty-five miles to the border," I said. "Can we make it in one run? Maybe losing a few head?"

Miguel shrugged. "With luck, señor, one can do anything."

Me, I was doing some studying, and it came to me that whatever was going to happen would happen fast now. Tomorrow night—or perhaps the next—we would be driving for the border. And we'd have the gold with us.

But I wasn't thinking of that gold, I was thinking of pa. My father, whom I had not seen for eight years, was somewhere out there in the darkness.

The question was: did he know I was here?

SEVEN

M iguel shook me awake an hour after midnight, and I sat
up, feeling the dampness caused by the nearness of the
Gulf. The fire was a glowing bed of coals and the coffee pot
was steaming. Gin was asleep, her head cushioned on her
saddle.

"It's quiet," Miguel said, "too damn' quiet."

He looked very bad this morning, his face still swollen,
and blood from an opened whip-cut tracing a way across his
cheek.

"We're going to make a run for the border," I said. "You
get your sleep."

He was dog-tired, and he hit the blankets and was asleep
before I could drink my coffee. He'd taken time to saddle my
dun before waking me, which was like him. I thought of his
wife back in Texas and knew that whatever else happened,
he must get back to her. And he would not go unless with
me. He was that loyal.

The cattle were resting and quiet. They'd had grass and

water a-plenty and were fixing to get fat. Or maybe they were stoking up for what was to come.

Among any bunch of cattle, as among humans, you will find a few staid, steady characters, and there were a couple of such steers in this herd that I'd been cultivating. These had been wild cattle; but cattle, horses, or men, no two are quite alike, and these I'd chosen showed a disposition to be friendly. It was in my mind that I might need a couple of steady steers, and these two I'd fed a few choice bunches of grass or leaves.

Truth of the matter was, I was scared. Both Gin and Miguel were looking to me, and I wasn't sure I was up to it. I had never been in a real shoot-out difficulty, and it worried me that I was trusted to handle whatever came.

Wind moaned in the brush. Finishing my coffee, I put aside my cup and, shoving the Henry into the boot, mounted up and rode out to the head, singing low. Water rustled along the shore of the inlet, sucking and whispering among the reeds and the old drift timbers. Once it spat a few drops of cold rain.

This time of night, I was thinking, would be the time to run. Herrara would have us watched, but on a cold, unpleasant night there might be a chance.

Twice I rode wide of the herd to get a better over-all look, and I rode with care, pistol to hand. There was nothing to see, less to hear.

But bit by bit something was shaping up in my mind. There was this long arm of the sea to the east of us, and that other wider arm to the west and south. We were on a point, with water on two sides. Dimly, I recalled some tracings pa had made in the earth at the back door of the cabin one day as he talked. It was like this point...down there on the very point he'd made a cross of some kind.

Tomorrow...I would go there tomorrow.

It was coming up to day when I turned back toward camp. The cattle were on their feet, most of them cropping grass. If what I thought proved true, we might be lighting a shuck out of this country come nighttime. And believe me, I wanted to be shut of it.

When I rode up to the fire I saw Gin was up and drinking coffee. How she'd managed to get her hair to looking like that, I don't know. She reached across the fire's edge to fill Miguel's cup...but it wasn't Miguel.

It was pa.

He was setting hunched up to the fire with a blanket over his shoulders and a cup of coffee held in both his hands. He looked thinner than I had ever seen him, his face honed down hard.

He looked up when I walked that dun into the fire's circle of light, and for a minute or two we just stared at each other like a couple of fools.

"Pa?" I said. It was all I could get out.

He got up, the blanket falling to the ground. He was a big man, even now with almost no flesh on him. He'd been that prisoner who escaped, and Lord knows how long he'd been mistreated in that prison.

"Son?" He had a hard time with the word. "Orlando?"

"It's been a long time, pa."

No words came to me, and it seemed he was no better off. He had left me a child, and found me a man. Swinging down, I trailed my reins and stepped out to face him.

He was taller than me, but raw-boned as he was now, he was no heavier than my one-eighty. He thrust out his hand and I took it. "You're strong," he said. "You were always strong."

"You've had some grub?"

"Coffee...just coffee, and some talk with Gin."

Gin, was it? He wasted no time getting down to cases. "You'd better eat," I said. "Come daybreak, we're going down to the Point."

"Ah?" he was pleased. "So you did remember?"

"Took me a while, but it was coming to me."

"Gin said you'd recognized the shelter—and the marker, too."

"You'd better sit down and wrap up," Gin advised. "You aren't well."

She put the blanket around him when he sat down and with a tiny prick of jealousy I couldn't help but think that if pa were shaved and fixed up they'd make a handsome pair.

I got out the frying pan and mixed up some sourdough, listening to them talk the while. He had the pleasant voice I'd remembered, and the easy way of moving. Glancing over at them, it came over me that pa was *here*...he was *alive*.

I'd been too stunned to take it in rightly before, and it was going to take some getting used to.

His eyes were on me as I shook up that bread, and I suppose he was wondering what sort of a man I'd become. But there was something else in his mind, too.

"You speak as if you'd had no schooling," he said. "Not that it's better or worse than most men speak out here."

"We'll have to talk to Caffrey," I said. "He used your money for his own self. I've been caring for myself at your old cabin since I was twelve." Looking up at him, I grinned. "With some help now and again from the Cherokees."

"I worried about Caffrey," pa said, "but I was in a hurry to get off. And that reminds me. We'd best get out of here. If they find me with you, you'll all be shot."

"Not without that gold," I said. "We came this far for it."

"There's some all ready to go," pa said. "I've taken it out myself. The rest—most of it—will take time."

Gin looked over at me. "Orlando, I think he's right. He's a sick man. The way his breathing sounds, he may be getting pneumonia."

The word had a dread sound, and it shook me. Miguel was sleeping, but it came on me then that we'd best move the cattle a little way, like to new bedding grounds, but hold them ready for a fast move when darkness came.

"Is that gold where it can be laid hands on?" I asked.

"It is."

"We'll move the cattle on to the end of the inlet and bed

down there, like for night. Short of midnight we'll make our run."

My mind was thinking ahead. Gin probably was making the right guess, for pa looked bad. He had been lying out in the brush without so much as a coat, just shirt and pants. Even his boots were worn through and soaked.

Leisurely, we rounded up the cattle, with pa keeping from sight in the brush, and we walked them on not more than a mile. Then, late afternoon, we built ourselves a new fire and settled down as if for the night.

Rounding up those placid steers I'd been keeping my eyes on, we brought them up to camp. Then, with pa resting, we waited the coming of night.

Miguel was restless. He never was far from his horse, and he worried himself until he was taut as a drumhead, watching the brush, listening, afraid something would go wrong before we could get away.

"I'm going into Guadalupe," I said to him. "We need a couple of horses."

There was no way he could deny that, although he wished to. We had no mount for pa, and if we made a run for it, we'd be riding from here clean to the border.

Miguel shrugged. "I think it is safe enough," he admitted reluctantly, "and we have reason to get horses."

Gin had money. She had more than I did, which wasn't much, so she turned over a hundred dollars to me and I saddled up the dun. Just before I left, I walked over to where pa was lying, with Gin setting beside him. No question but he looked bad.

"You take it easy," I said. "I'll get two, three horses and come back."

"What about pack horses? For the gold?"

"Packs would make the Mexicans mighty curious, so I figured on steers. Nobody will pay any attention to the herd."

"They'll be seen."

"Maybe...but with horns moving, and the dust, the

shifting around of the animals...I think we've got a chance."

It was a mite over four miles to Guadalupe, and not even a dozen buildings when I got there, most of them adobe. There was a *cantina*, a closed-up store, and the office of the *alcalde*, with a jail behind it. The rest were scattered houses and one warehouse.

In a corral were several rough-looking horses, but nobody was around. The air was chill, offering rain. At the hitchrail of the *cantina* stood more horses, three of them led stock. I tied up the dun and went inside.

It was a low, dark room with a bar and several tables. Three men were at the bar, two of them standing together, their backs to me. A broad-shouldered Mexican with a sombrero hanging down his back by the chin-strap, and crossed cartridge belts on his chest, stood at the end of the bar, a bottle before him. He looked like a Herrara man to me. The other two were lounging with a bottle between them. The Herrara man was obviously interested in them.

Walking up to the bar, I put my elbows on it and ordered a beer.

The operator of the *cantina* accepted my money and flashed a brief smile at me, but in his eyes I thought there was a warning, an almost imperceptible gesture toward the Herrara man, if such he was.

"Holding cattle outside of town," I said suddenly. "We've played out our horses. Know where I can buy a couple, cheap?"

For maybe a minute nobody made any sign they'd heard me, and then the man next to me said, "I have three horses, and I will sell—but not cheap."

It was the Tinker.

Without turning my head, I picked up my bottle of beer and emptied the rest of it into my glass. "Another," I said, gesturing.

"I saw them," I added, "at the rail. They are fit for buzzards."

"They are good horses," the Tinker protested. "I had not considered selling them until you spoke. The buckskin...there is a horse!"

"I'll give you eight dollars for him," I said, and tasted my beer.

For half an hour we argued and debated back and forth. Finally, I said, "All right, twelve dollars for the buckskin, fifteen for the bay—the paint I do not want."

The Tinker and his silent companion, at whom I had not dared to look for fear of drawing attention to him, seemed to be growing drunk. The Tinker clapped me on the shoulder. "You are a good man," he said drunkenly, "a very good man! You need the horses—all right, I shall sell you the horses. You may have all three for forty dollars and a good meal...it is my last price."

I shrugged. "All right—but if you want the meal, come to camp. Forty dollars is all the money I have."

There on the bar I paid it to him in *pesos*, and we walked outside, the Tinker talking drunkenly. The Herrara man's eyes were drilling into my back.

"He's watching us," the Tinker said as I stopped to look over the horses.

Straightening up, I looked into the eyes of the other man—Jonas Locklear. "Cortina had me turned loose," he said, "on condition I get out of the country. He didn't want Herrara to know for the present."

Mounting up, we rode swiftly from the town. By the time we reached camp it was near to sunset. Pa was up, had a gun strapped on that Miguel had taken from our gear, and he was watching the sun.

"The only place they can watch us from," he said, "is that dune. It looks over the whole country around here. It's over seventy feet high, and in this country that's a mountain—along the coast, that is. If we wait about ten or fifteen minutes, the sun will be shining right in the eyes of anybody watching from that dune. That's when we'll go for the gold."

97

We now mustered six rifles, a good force by anybody's count, for Gin could shoot—or said she could, and I believed her.

We made beds ready, built up the fire, and put coffee on, and grub. Miguel was cooking.

When the sun got low enough, Pa, the Tinker and me took a few canvas bags we'd brought along a-purpose, and with two steers we headed off into the brush. One of the steers showed old marks that looked like he'd been used as a draft animal sometime in the past. Both were easily handled.

As we walked, pa said, "I dove for this gold, got it out of the sand on the bottom. Most of the hull is still intact, and most of the gold will be inside, but I brought up enough to make it pay. We'll take this and run; then we'll wait for things to simmer down, and come back."

Then pa told us some about how things were in Mexico. Right about this time Cortina had gathered a lot of power to him, but he was dependent on some of the lieutenants he had, of whom Herrara was one. The situation was changing rapidly, and it had changed several times over in the period of the last thirty years. Even in the last six or seven years there had been power shifts and changes, and changing relationships with the United States.

Not many years before, a Mexican cavalry detachment had crossed the border to protect Brownsville from a Mexican bandit, a fact known to few Americans except those in the immediate vicinity.

In the northern provinces of Mexico there was much division of feeling as to the United States, and the northern country had many friends south of the border. North of the border many citizens of Mexican extraction had fought against Mexico for Texas. It was difficult to draw a line, and there was a constant struggle in process for power below the border.

Pa told me some of this, and some I'd had from Jonas while riding south when there had been time to talk.

Pa led us in such a way as to keep bushes between us

and the dune he thought was the lookout post, until we arrived right down on the shore of the inlet. There on the point, right where I'd planned to look, there was where pa stopped.

"The ship," he said to me, "lies off there, in no more than five fathoms of water."

He glanced over his shoulder at the sun, then stopped and took hold of a tuft of grass and pulled on it; he caught hold of another bunch with the other hand. A big chunk of sod lifted out like a trap door, and in a hollowed-out place underneath was a tin pail and several cans, loaded with gold.

There was no time to lose. Working as swiftly as we could, we sacked it up, for the sun was going down and in a few minutes we'd stand out like sore thumbs out there on that point. Tying the sacks two and two, we hung them over the backs of the steers, and then replaced the sod. We started back as if driving two straying steers.

As darkness came we clustered around the fire, eating. Miguel and Jonas finished first and, mounting up, went out to circle the cattle. The rest of us went through the motions of going to bed. One by one the others moved off into the darkness, but Gin and me, we still sat by the fire and I stoked the flames a mite higher.

"He's quite a man," she said suddenly.

"Pa?"

"Yes. I've never known anyone quite like him."

Me, I hadn't anything to say. I didn't know enough about my own father, and there'd been little time for talking. Also, as the time drew near we were getting worrisome about what we had to do.

You bed down a bunch of steers and they'll finally settle down to dozing and chewing their cuds; but after a while, close to midnight or about there, they'll all stand up and stretch, crop grass a bit, and then lie down again. That was the time we'd picked to move them—catch them on their feet so there'd be less disturbance.

Finally we left the fire, adding some more fuel. I rigged

some branches nearby so they'd sort of fall into the fire as others burned, giving anybody watching an idea the fire was being fed, time to time.

Away from the firelight, I moved up to my dun in the darkness and tightened the cinch. "You got it in you to run," I said, "you better have at it tonight."

We waited...and we waited. And those fool steers, they just lay there chewing and sleeping. Then, of a sudden, an old range cow stood up. In a minute or two there were a dozen on their feet, and then more.

Moving mighty easy, we started to push them. Miguel was off to one side to get them started north, and Jonas had gone up the other side.

We pushed them, and a few of them began, reluctantly, to move out. It took us a while to get them started and lined out, and we did it without any shouting or hollering.

We walked them easy for about a mile, then we began to move them a little faster. Not until we had about three miles behind us did we give it to them.

It was a wild ride. I'll say this for Gin, she was right in there with us, riding side-saddle as always, but riding like any puncher and doing her job. Only I noticed she was keeping an eye on pa, too.

It made me sore, only I didn't want to admit it. I told myself somebody had to keep an eye on him, the shape he was in. Nevertheless, I was a mite jealous, too. I reckon it's the male in a man...he sees a pretty woman like that and wants to latch onto her. She was a good bit older than me, of course, though a whole sight younger than pa.

We had those cattle lined out and we kept them going. After a ways we'd slow down to give them a breather, but not so slow that they could get to thinking what was happening to them. Then we'd speed them up a little. After six miles or so, the Tinker, he swung in beside me. "We'd best hang back, you and me," he said, "sort of a rear guard."

The night wore on.

Once when we came up to water we let them line out

along the creek bank and drink. We had ten miles behind us then, but by daybreak we hoped to have a few more, because it wouldn't take free-riding horsemen long to catch up, and when they did there'd be hell to pay.

We had managed to keep in sight those steers carrying the gold. We'd lashed that gold in place, throwing a good packing hitch over it, and there was small danger of it falling off—nevertheless, somebody always had an eye on that gold.

The dark skies began to gray. We were more than half-way there, but we still had miles to go. The cattle had slowed to a walk. They'd have been plenty angry if they hadn't been so tired.

Pa looked awful. His face was drawn and pale, but he was riding as well as any of us. His eyes were sunk into his skull, and they looked bigger than anybody's eyes should.

We pushed on, walking them now, trying to create no more dust than we had to.

There was a place east of Matamoras where it looked like the border swung further south, and so would be nearer to us. We turned the herd that way, skirting a sort of lake or tidewater pool.

It was just shy of noon and we were within five or six miles of the border when they came at us.

It was about that time, just before they hit us, that I had my brain-storm. It came to me of a sudden and, saying nothing to anyone but the Tinker, I rode up to Gin.

"Look, you and pa take those two steers and you move out ahead. If we have to make a fight of it, we'll do it better without having to think of you."

"I can fight," pa said.

His looks shocked me, and he was coughing a lot and his forehead was wet with sweat. His cheeks were a sickly white, but I was sure he was carrying a lot of fever in him.

"Do like I say," I insisted. "You two light out and head for the border. If we have to, we'll make a fight of it and cover for you. With that money, you can help us out if we should get caught."

"If you aren't killed," pa said.

"I'm too durned ornery to die," I said. "Anyway, we got to go back to Tennessee and talk to Caffrey, you and me together."

Gin convinced him, and they taken those two steers and drove them off ahead of the herd.

They hadn't been gone more than a few minutes when we saw that dust cloud come a-helling up the road after us. The Tinker and me, we just looked at each other, and then the lead began to come our way. I was sort of glad, for I'd no wish to start shooting at folks when I ain't sure of their plans.

That old Henry came up to my shoulder sweet and pretty, and my first shot taken a man right out of the saddle. At least, I think it was my shot.

We both fired, and then we turned tail and got away from there, racing past the herd like Jonas and Miguel were doing.

We started to swing the herd and in no time at all had them turned between us and those men after us. We tried to stampede them back into those fellows, but only a few of them started—the rest were too almighty confused.

All of us were shooting, riding and shooting, and then they cut around both sides of the herd at us and our horses were too blown to run. We made our fight right there.

Dropping off my horse, I swung him around and shot across the saddle. There were guns going off all around me, and I'd no time to be scared.

"'Lando!" the Tinker shouted, and grabbed at me. "Ride and run!"

Both of us jumped for the saddle, and as we did so I saw a man wearing a black suit come out of that bunch. He had a shotgun in his hands, and as Jonas turned toward his horse he let him have both barrels.

Miguel was down, and now Jonas, and it needed no sawbones to tell me Jonas was dead. Before I could more than try a shot at that rider in the black suit, he was gone.

But not until I'd seen him.

It was Franklyn Deckrow. The Tinker had seen him, too.

We lit out. We were running all out when I felt my horse bunch up under me, and then he went head over heels into the sand, pitching me wide over his head.

Last I saw was the Tinker giving one wild glance my way, and then he was racing away.

From that look on his face, I was sure he figured me for a dead man.

Reaching out, I grabbed for my Henry, which had fallen from my hand. A boot came down hard on my knuckles, and when I looked up Antonio Herrara was looking down at me. And from the expression of those flat black eyes, I knew I'd bought myself some trouble.

It was going to be a long time before I saw Texas again...if ever.

EIGHT

The bitter days edged slowly by, and weeks passed into years, and then the years were gone, and still I remained a prisoner.

By day I worked like the slave I'd become, and was fed like an animal, and by night I slept on a bed of filthy straw and dreamed of a day when I would be free.

Always I was alone, alone within the hollow shell of my mind, for outside the small world in which I lived with labor, sweat, and frightful heat, no one knew that I lived, nor was there anyone about me to whom I could talk.

The others with whom I worked were Indians—Yaquis brought to this place from Sonora, men self-contained and bitter as I, yet knowing nothing of me, nor trusting anyone beyond their own small group.

A thousand times I planned escape, a thousand times the plans crumbled. Doors that seemed about to open for me remained closed, guards who showed weakness were replaced. My hands became curved to grip the handles of pick, shovel, or mattock. My shoulders bulged with muscle put there by swinging a heavy sledge. Naturally of great strength, each day of work made it greater, building roads, working in the mines, clearing mesquite-covered ground.

Sometimes alone in my rock-walled cell I thought back to that first day when, in a square adobe room, I was questioned by Herrara. My wrists bound cruelly tight, I stood before him.

He stood with his feet apart, his sombrero tipped back, and those flat black eyes looked into mine. He smiled then, showing even white teeth; he was a handsome man in a savage way. "You put a gun upon me," he said, and struck me across the face with his quirt.

It was the beginning of pain.

"There is gold. Tell me where it is, and you may yet go free."

He lied...he had no thought to let me go, only to see me suffer and die.

"The gold is gone. They took it with them."

"I think you lie," he said and, almost negligently, he lashed me again across the face with the quirt, and the lash cut deep. I tasted my blood upon my cut lips, and I knew the beginning of hatred.

That was the beginning of questioning, but only the beginning. There was gold. He knew it and was hungry for it, as the others had been before him. The original commandant, whose name I never knew, had been his uncle. In the telling, the amount of gold supposedly hidden on the shore had grown to a vast amount.

To tell him was to die, and I lived to kill him, so I told him nothing. After each questioning I was taken to a cell and left there, and each time I feared I would die; but deep within me the days tempered a kind of steel I had not known was there.

Herrara I would remember, and another man, too. I would remember Franklyn Deckrow, who had betrayed us to them, and who had killed Jonas, his brother-in-law. It was something to live for.

And I would live. No matter what, I would survive so that these men might die.

No help could come to me, for they believed me dead. Jonas had fallen, and Miguel too, although he might have somehow gotten away. They had forced me to bury Jonas, but Miguel's body was nowhere around. I hoped for him. But the Tinker had looked back and seen me lying there, and I knew he believed me dead.

Suddenly, one night, I was moved. Out of a sound sleep I was shaken awake, jerked to my feet and led away. Herrara rode beside me.

"Your friends do not give up," he said, "and they have powerful friends in Mexico, so we must take you where you will never be found."

The place to which they took me was a ranch owned by an outlaw named Flores, an outlaw who raided Texas ranches for their stock and so was ignored by the law of the province.

Duty called Herrara away to the south, so the beatings ended, but I was put to work among the Yaqui slaves. Most of the Yaqui prisoners had been sent away to work in the humid south where they soon died. Only a few were kept in the north.

The work was preferable to the cell, and I gloried in my growing strength. We were fed corn and *frijoles* and good beef, all of which was cheap enough, and they wanted my strength for the work I could do.

A dozen times I tried to smuggle messages across the border. Twice they were found and I was beaten brutally.

"Tell me," Herrara said to me on one of his sudden visits, "tell me where is the gold and you shall have a horse and your freedom." But I did not tell.

Herrara had become powerful. The outlaws supported him and he protected them and derived income from their raids into Texas. Night after night men rode away from the Flores ranch and raided over the border, returning with cattle, horses, and women.

No other Mexican came to the ranch to visit, and I gathered the outlaws were hated by those who lived nearby, but they were people cut off from authority who could do nothing.

When I looked down at my hands, I saw them calloused and scarred, but powerful. My shoulders and arms were heavy with muscle, and my mind, sharpened by endless observation and planning, was cunning as an animal's is cunning.

No day passed without its plan for escape, no possible opportunity went unnoticed by me. Always my senses were alert for the moment.

Then came another Herrara visit. The heavy oaken door grated against the stone, and he stepped inside. He held a pistol and a heavy whip, the cat-o'-nine-tails which is used aboard ship. Behind him in the doorway were two men with guns.

"It is the end," he said. "I shall wait no longer. Tonight you will tell me, for if you do not, these"—he held up the whip—"will take out your eyes."

· The cat hung from his hand by its stubby wooden handle, and from its end dangled nine strips of rawhide, each with a tip wrapped in wire. It was a whip that could cut a man to ribbons, or bite at his eyes, cutting them from his head in a bloody mess.

And in that moment I knew that I could no longer wait. I must kill him and be killed.

He moved toward me, and I remained where I was, crouched in the corner with one heel braced against the wall, ready to lunge at him. My thick forearms rested upon my knees, and I waited, watching him like the cornered animal I had become.

We were at a smaller ranch, half a mile from Las Cuevas, the headquarters of Flores. It was November 19, 1875. The date is one I shall never forget.

A mistake was made that night, and upon such mistakes do men's lives depend; by such mistakes are men's lives lost—or saved. Outside my cell, beyond the walls about the ranch, beyond the border even, events had marched forward, and tonight men rode in darkness, moving along the cactus-lined trails.

As Herrara came toward me, he had his pistol ready, for he was a clever man and knew what must be in my mind. The whip was poised for a blow, but I was hard to get at, for the corner was a partial protection.

My tongue went to my lips. Within me burned a kind of cold fury, welling up from the deep hatreds that had grown within me, until nothing mattered but my hands upon his throat.

He would strike me. His bullet would tear into my flesh, and perhaps the bullets of those others in the doorway, but my hands must reach his throat. These hands that only a day or so before had bent and twisted an iron horseshoe—these hands must reach that throat and lock there. Surely, I would be killed, but surely I should kill him first.

He flipped the whip at me, but I did not move. He lifted the whip to strike downward, and he brought it down hard over my head and shoulders, but still I did not move. Suddenly his own anger burst within him, the hatred of me because I kept him from the wealth he wanted and the position it would buy, the hatred of me for holding out so long against him.

His lips curled from his teeth and the whip drew back for a mighty blow at my face. Those wire-twisted whipends would tear at my eyes. His own hatred had mastered him—I saw it in his face.

Suddenly, from outside there was a crash of gunfire, the race of pounding hoofs, shrill Texas yells.

The men at the door wheeled and ran toward the court. Even Herrara was caught, gripped by shock in the middle of his blow. And in that instant I leaped.

My left hand gripped the gun-wrist, my right seized his throat, not a grip around the neck, but the far more deadly grip of the Adam's apple and the throat itself.

His gun exploded, but the muzzle had been turned aside,

and the roar was lost in the concussions of the shots outside. I smashed him back bodily against the stone wall with stunning force. My right hand gripping his throat held him on tip-toes against the stone, and my other hand gripping his gun-wrist ground his knuckles against the roughness of the stone wall.

Brutally, I ground the flesh against the stone, rasping it back and forth until he struggled to scream and his fingers could no longer grip the gun.

I released my hold upon his throat and stepped back. He struck weakly at me with the cat, but then, my feet wide, I hit with my left fist, then with my right, rolling my shoulders for the power it gave. One fist struck his ribs, crushing them; the other his face.

His head bounced against the wall, and glassy-eyed he started to fall toward me. I struck him again, and when he fell forward that time I knew that he was dead.

Quickly, I stripped off his gun belt and picked his pistol from the floor.

The passage outside the door was empty, and I ran along it, turned down another, and was in the living quarters of the ranch house. A door stood open, as it had been left when the shooting called the men out, and I smashed through it.

The room was empty and still. My footsteps padded on the bare floor as I crossed to the gun case. Picking up a chair with one hand, I swung it and smashed the glass. I reached in for a shotgun and filled my pockets with shells.

A Henry rifle was there, and I took that also, and two belts of cartridges that hung from a chair. And then as I turned away I saw a familiar sight. In the corner of the gun cabinet was my old Walch Navy .36 with the initials C.B. scratched on it. Quickly, I took it up and thrust it into my waistband with another pistol that lay there.

No one appeared in the passage as I ran, and I went through the door to the long veranda outside. There I stopped in the shadows.

Mounted men were racing back and forth, and the red lances of gunfire stabbed the darkness. A Texas yell broke out, and a shot caught a Mexican upon a balcony. He fell head-long from it and landed nearby. The rider wheeled his horse, and in that instant he saw me.

The pistol swung at me to fire and I shouted, *"No!* I'm an *American!"*

He held his pistol on me. "Who are you?" His voice rang with authority.

"A prisoner. They've held me six years."

"Six years?"

A horse was tied to the hitch-rail and he jerked loose the tie-rope. Heavier firing sounded outside the court. *"Come! And be quick!"*

He raced from the court to where other Texas riders were milling. "Wrong place!" A man shouted at the rider beside me. "Flores's place is half a mile up the road!"

"There are two hundred men there!" I yelled at them.

The man beside me said, "Let's go!" And he led the racing retreat at a dead run down the valley.

After a mile or two they slowed to a canter, then to a walk. I glanced at the stars, and there was the North Star, beckoning us on.

"They'll be after us," the man beside me said, and there was no time for questions.

Closely we rode on, and fast, for the Rio Grande lay miles to the north. The night was cool, and the air fresh on my face. Sometimes when we passed close to a rock face we could feel the heat still held from the day's hot sun.

We slowed to a walk again, and the man I rode beside turned in his saddle and looked at me.

"Six years, you say?"

As briefly as possible, I explained. Not about the gold, exactly, but enough to let him know they had wanted to learn a secret I alone knew. When I mentioned Herrara, he nodded grimly. "He's one I'd like to find myself."

111

"Do not waste your time," I said. "From now on you need pay him no mind."

He glanced at me and I said, "He was using a whip on me when you came shooting into the patio, and his men rushed away."

"He is dead, you think?"

"He is dead. Without a doubt, he is dead."

"My name is McNelly," the rider said then. "These are Texas Rangers."

Thirty of them had crossed the river to strike a blow at the outlaws who were raiding ranches and stealing cattle north of the border—and sometimes south of it, as well.

Las Cuevas had long been the outlaws' headquarters, and it was Las Cuevas for which the Rangers had aimed. But mistakenly they were led to a ranch that belonged to the Las Cuevas owner, only a short distance away from the main ranch buildings. It was that mistake that had saved my life.

At the Rio Grande the riders turned on command. The outlaws were not far behind. "You, Sackett," the captain said, "go on across the border. You've had trouble enough."

"If you'll grant me the pleasure, Cap'n," I said, "I'll stay. There's men in that crowd who have struck me and beaten me, and I owe them a little. Besides," I added, "I carried off their shotgun. It is only fair that I return the loads from the shells."

Here at the river the air was still cooler because of the dampness rising from the water—and it was free air. For the first time in years I was out in the night, with free air all about me.

The outlaws came with a rush, sure they would catch the Rangers at the border before they got across the river, but they were met with a blast of gunfire that lanced the night with darting flame. One rider toppled from his saddle, and his fall as much as our fire turned their retreat into a rout. They vanished into the mesquite.

Several Rangers rode out to look at the body, and I followed McNelly. "Well," I said, "seems to me if you had to kill only one, you got the right one. That there is Flores himself."

We swam the river back to the Texas side and I followed on to their camp, which was on the bank of a creek a few miles back from the river.

Reckon I looked a sight. My shirt was in rags and the only pants I had were some castoffs they'd given me when my own played out. There I stood, bare-footed and loaded down with guns.

"You'd better let us stand you an outfit," McNelly commented dryly. "You're in no shape to go anywhere in that outfit."

They were good boys, those Rangers were, and they rigged me out. Then, to raise some cash, I sold one of them my pistol for six dollars—it was the spare I'd picked up (I'd come away with three); and I sold the shotgun for twelve to McNelly himself. The Captain had taken Flores's gold- and silver-plated pistol off the body—it was a rarely beautiful weapon.

The horse I'd ridden across the border was a handsome, upstanding roan.

"Anybody asks you for the bill of sale for that horse," McNelly commented, "you refer them to me."

The first thing I did was to head for the creek and take a long bath, getting shut of my old clothes at the time. When I lit out for Rio Grande City, come daybreak, I felt like a different man.

Yet being free wasn't what it might have been. First off, I didn't know where to go. McNelly had heard nothing of my pa, and only remembered some talk of Jonas Locklear being dead several years back. What had become of his land, he didn't know.

So there I was, a free man with no place to go, with a rightful share in gold that might have already been spent. But something I did own, if I could find them. I owned a mare and a mule colt.

I showed up in Brownsville wearing shirt and jeans that

didn't fit, a pair of boots that hurt my feet, and a worn-out Mexican sombrero. Dark as I was and wearing cartridge belts crossed over my chest, I even looked like a Mexican.

I walked into a *cantina* and leaned on the bar, and when the bartender ignored me I reached out my Henry and laid it across to touch the back bar.

"I want a whiskey," I said, "and I want it now. You going to give it to me, or do I take it after I put a knot on your head?"

He looked at me and then he looked at that rifle and he set the bottle out on the bar. "We don't cater to Mexicans in here," he said.

"You do wrong," I told him. "I'm no Mex, but I've known some mighty fine ones. They run about true to form with us north of the border—some good and some bad."

"Sorry," he said. "I thought you were a Mexican."

"Pour me a drink," I said, "and then go back and shut up."

He poured me the drink and walked away down the bar. Two tough-looking cowhands were sizing me up, considering how much opposition I'd offer if trouble started, but I wasn't interested in a row. So I just plain ignored them. Anyway, I was listening to talk at a table behind me.

"He's wise," one man was saying. "He hasn't squatted on range the way most have done. Captain King clears title on every piece he buys. That's why he's held off on that Locklear outfit—there's a dispute over the title. Deckrow claims it, but his sister-in-law disputes the claim."

"Bad blood between Deckrow and her husband, too. It'll come to a shooting."

"Not unless Deckrow shoots him in the back," I said, "that's the way he killed Jonas Locklear."

Well, now. I'd turned and spoken aloud without really meaning to, and every face in the room turned toward me.

One of the men at the table looked at me coldly. "That's poor talk. Deckrow's a respected man in Texas."

"He wouldn't be the first who didn't deserve it," I said.

"You see him, you tell him I said he was a back-shooter. Tell him I said he shot Jonas Locklear in the back, and Deckrow was riding with Mexican outlaws at the time."

There wasn't a friendly face in the *cantina*, except maybe for the other man at that table.

"And who might you be?" he asked quietly. "We'd like to tell him who spoke against him."

"The name is Orlando Sackett," I said, "and I'll speak against him any time I get the chance.... Jonas," I added, "was a friend of mine."

"Orlando Sackett," the man said thoughtfully. "The only other Sackett I know besides Falcon was killed down in Mexico, five or six years ago."

"You heard wrong. I ain't dead, nor about to be."

Finishing my drink, I turned and walked out of the place and went across the street to a restaurant.

A few minutes after, a slender blue-eyed man came in and sat down not far from me. He didn't look at me at all, and that was an odd thing, because almost everybody else at least glanced my way.

In Rio Grande City I'd gotten myself a haircut and had my beard shaved off. I still held to a mustache, like most men those days, but it was trimmed careful. In the six years below the border I'd taken on weight, and while I was no taller than five-ten, I now weighed two hundred and ten pounds, most of it in my chest and shoulders. Folks looked at me, all right.

As I ate, I kept an eye on that blue-eyed man, who was young and lean-faced and wore a tied-down gun. Presently another man came in and sat down beside him, his back to me. When he turned around a few minutes later and he looked at me, I saw he was Duncan Caffrey.

He'd changed some. His face looked like it always did, but he was big and strong-looking. His eyes were a lot harder than I recalled, and when he put his hand on the back of the other man's chair I noticed the knuckles were scarred and broken. He'd been doing a lot of fighting. Reminded me of

115

what the Tinker had said about the knuckles of Jem Mace, that champion fighter who'd trained him.

Caffrey looked hard at me, and he sort of frowned and looked away, and suddenly it came on me that he wasn't sure. True, I was a whole lot heavier than when he'd last seen me, and a lot darker except where the beard was shaved off, and even that had caught some sun riding down from Rio Grande City.

When I stood up and paid for my supper I saw in the mirror what was wrong. The mustache changed me a good bit, and the scars even more. I had forgotten the scars. There were three of them, two along my cheek and one on my chin, all made from the cuts of that quirt, which had cut like a knife into my flesh, and no stitches taken in the cuts.

Outside on the street a sudden thought came to me. If that blue-eyed man was a killer, and if Caffrey was pointing me out to him, then I'd better dust out. With my hands I was all right, but I hadn't shot a six-shooter, except for the other day, not in six years.

Riding out of town, I headed east, then circled and took the north road. A few days after, I pulled up at the *jacal* where I'd left the mare.

A young woman came to the door, shading her eyes at me. She looked shabby and tired. The little boy who stood beside her stared at me boldly, but I thought they were both frightened.

"Do you not remember me, señora? I rode from here many years ago—with Miguel and Señor Locklear."

There seemed to be a flicker of recognition in her eyes then, but all she said was, "Go away. Miguel is dead."

"Dead, señora?"

"*Si.*" Her eyes flickered around as if she were afraid of being observed. "He returned from Mexico, and then one day he did not come back to me. He was shot out on the plains— by *bandidos.*"

"Ah?" I wondered about those *bandidos* and about Franklyn Deckrow. Then I changed the subject. "When I was

116

here I left a mare that was to have a colt. You promised to see to the birth and care for it."

Her eyes warmed. "I remember, señor."

"The colt...is it here?"

The boy started to interrupt, but she spoke quickly to him in Spanish. I now spoke the tongue well, but they were not close to me and I missed the words.

"It is here, señor. Manuel will get it."

"Wait." I looked at the boy. "You have ridden the colt?"

"The mule, señor? *Si*, I have ridden him." There was no friendliness in his eyes. He was all of eleven or twelve, but slight of build.

"Does he run, then? Like the wind?"

Excitement came into his eyes and he spoke with enthusiasm. "*Si*, señor. He runs."

Juana came a step from the *jacal*. "He loves the mule," she said. "I am afraid he loves it too much. I always told him you would come for it."

"You told him I would come back?"

"*Si*, señor. Miguel did not believe you were dead. He never believed it. But he was the only one. Although the señora—Señora Sackett—she sometimes thought you were alive."

"Señora Sackett?"

"Your father's wife, señor. The sister of Señor Locklear."

So Gin had married my father. She was my stepmother now. Well, thinking back, I could not be surprised. From the first, there had been something between them.

Juana came out to my horse as the boy walked reluctantly away to get the mule. "There has been much trouble," she said. "Señor Deckrow lets us to live here, but he warned us never to talk to strangers, and he said if you ever came back, to send Manuel at once to tell him."

Just then my horse's head came up and I looked around, and there stood the mule colt.

No question but what it was a mule. It was tall, longer in the body than most mules, it seemed, and with long, slim legs. But it was a mule, almost a buckskin in color, and like enough to any mule I'd ever seen.

You could tell by the way he followed that boy that there was a good feeling between them. But when I walked over, he stretched his nose to me.

"And the mare?"

"Wolves, señor, when this one was small. If I had not come upon them, he would be dead also."

Rubbing the mule's neck, I considered the situation. "Manuel," I said, "I think you and Juana should come away from here. I think you should go to San Antonio, or somewhere. You'll need to have schooling."

"How? We have no money. We have no way to go. We have only our goats and a few chickens."

"You have horses?"

"No, señor. The horses belong to Señor Deckrow."

"Ride them, anyway, and you two come away to San Antonio." I paused. "If Deckrow hears you have talked to me, there may be trouble. Besides, I want a boy who can ride the mule...I mean who can race him. Could you do that, Manuel?"

His eyes sparkled, but he said seriously, "Sí, I could do it. He runs very fast, señor."

"He's bred for it," I said. "Can you go tonight?"

"What of the goats?"

"Goats," I said, "can get along. Leave them."

We didn't waste time. They'd little enough to take, and Manuel taken my horse and went out and caught up a couple of ponies in no time. He was a hand with a rope, which I wasn't. Lately I'd begun to think I wasn't a hand with anything, although all the way from Brownsville to the ranch I practiced with that Walch Navy, which I fancied beyond other guns.

The trail we chose was made by Kansas-bound cattle. Seemed to me I owed Miguel something, and I did not trust that Deckrow. So I'd be killing two birds with one stone by escorting Manuel and his mother to San Antone and getting Manuel to ride my mule for me.

"You think that mule can beat this horse?" I asked Manuel.

"Of a certainty," he replied coolly. "He can run, this mule."

So we laid it out between us to race to a big old cottonwood we could see away up ahead, maybe three-quarters of a mile off. On signal, we taken off.

Now that Mexican horse was a good cutting horse and trained to start fast. Moreover, it was an outlaw's horse, and an outlaw can't afford not to have the best horse under him that he can lay hands on. That roan took off with a bound and within fifty yards he was leading by two lengths, and widening the distance fast. We were halfway to that cottonwood before that mule got the idea into his head that he was in a race.

By the time we'd covered two-thirds of the distance we were running neck-and-neck, and then that mule just took off and left us.

Oakville was the town where I decided to make my play, and by the size of my bankroll it was going to be a small one.

When you came to sizing it up, Oakville wasn't a lot of town, there being less than a hundred people in it, but it had the name of being a contentious sort of place. Forty men were killed there in the ten years following the War Between the States. It lay right on the trail up from the border and a lot of Kansas cattle went through there, time to time.

When we came riding into town I told Manuel and his ma to find a place to put up, and I gave them a dollar.

It was a quiet day in town. A couple of buckboards stood on the street, and four or five horses stood three-legged at the hitch-rails. When I pushed through the bat-wing doors and went up to the bar, there was only one man in the place aside from the bartender. He was a long, thin man with a reddish mustache and a droll, quizzical expression to his eyes.

"Buy you a drink?" I suggested.

He looked at me thoughtfully. "Don't mind if I do." And then he said, "Passin' through?"

"Mostly," I said, "but what I'd like to rustle up is a horse race. I've got a Mex woman and her boy to care for."

He glanced at me, and I said, "Her husband stood by me in a fight below the border."

"Killed?"

"Uh-huh. They've kinfolk in San Antone."

He tasted his whiskey and said nothing. When he finished his drink he bought me one. "Lend you twenty dollars," he suggested. "I'll meet up with you again sometime."

"What I want is a horse race." I lowered my voice. "I've got me a fast mule. If I can get a bet, I could double the ten dollars I've got. Might even get odds, betting on a mule."

He walked to the door and looked over the bat-wings at the mule, which was tethered alongside my roan. Then he came back and leaned on the bar and tossed off his whiskey.

"Man east of town has him a fast horse. Come sundown he'll ride in. You mind if I bet a little?"

"Welcome it. You from here?"

"Beeville. Only I come over this way, time to time, on business. I'm buying cattle."

That man had him a horse, all right, and that horse had plenty of speed, but my mule just naturally left him behind, although Manuel was holding him up a mite, like I suggested.

That ten dollars made up to twenty, and the cattle buyer handed me twenty more. "Don't worry," he said, "I made a-plenty."

He looked at me thoughtfully. "You ever been over to Beeville? There's a lot of money floating around over there and they're fixing to have some horse races come Saturday. If you're of a mind to, we might just traipse over that way. It's somewhat out of your way, but not to speak of."

"I'm a man needs money," I said. "I don't mind if I do."

"They're fixing to have a prize fight, too. Mostly Irish folks over there—Beeville was settled by Irish immigrants back about 1830 or so." Then he went on, "Powerful pair of shoulders you got there. You ever do any fighting?"

"Don't figure on it," I said, "not unless I come up to a couple of men I'm looking for."

"Gambler over there," he said, "brought in a fighter. He nearly killed the local pride, so they're drumming up another fight to get some of their own back."

"I'm no fighter," I said, "not unless I'm pushed."

"Too bad. A horse race is all right, but if you could whip this Dun Caffrey, you could—"

"I'm pushed," I said. "I'm really feeling pushed. Did you say Dun Caffrey?"

"That was the name. He's good, make no mistake, and the Bishop is his backer."

Right then I recalled those scarred and broken knuckles I'd seen on Caffrey that time down on the border. But who would ever think Dun Caffrey would turn into a prize fighter? Still, he was strong, and he handled himself well. And maybe I'd been just lucky that day down in the field when I broke him up.

Those days a saloon was not only a place for drinking. It was a meeting place, a club, a place where business deals were made, a betting parlor, and an exchange for information. If you wanted to know about a trail, or whether the Indians were out, or who had cattle for sale, you went to a saloon.

"You make your bets on the fight," I said, "but you don't need to mention any name—just tell him I'm from Oakville, or just up from Mexico."

This cattle buyer's name was Doc Halloran, and he sized up to me like a canny one. "Dun Caffrey has won six fights in Texas, and more than that in Louisiana and Mississippi. He's a bruiser, but no fool. He's a gambler, and a companion of gamblers."

"That's as may be, but if you'll back me, I'll have at him."

"Are you in shape?"

"Six years at hard labor in a Mexican prison," I said. "Yes, I'm in shape."

121

We went into Beeville by the back streets and Doc Halloran took me to his own house. When I got there I stretched out for a rest. Juana and Manuel, they were there, too. Doc went out to rustle some bets on a horse race and to enter my mule. And he went to talk up this fight, too.

About sundown Manuel came back from rousting around. He was a mighty serious Mexican boy. "There is great trouble, señor," he said. "I think we have been followed to this place, for Señor Deckrow is here. He rides in his carriage with the señorita, but there are many men with him."

So I sat up on the edge of the bed and looked down at my thick, work-hardened hands, thinking. It was scarcely possible they had found us so quickly, nor would Deckrow be likely to bring the señorita, as Manuel had said. That would be Marsha, the little one.

Only she would be close to twenty now, and almost an old maid, for a time when girls married at sixteen or seventeen.

"I do not think they had followed us, *amigo*. It may be they go to San Antonio. He would want riders for protection. It is said there are many thieves."

Sitting on the edge of the bed after he left, I turned my mind again to the situation. Maybe this was the showdown that had to come sooner or later. Dun Caffrey would be here, Deckrow...how many others?

Doc Halloran came back before midnight. His long, friendly face was serious, and he stood looking down at me. "Well, the fight is set," he said. "And we've got the mule entered in the race, but I think we've bit off more than we can chew."

"What happened?"

He touched his tongue to his lips. "I bet five thousand on the mule, but they roped me in and egged me on, and I went over my head. I've bet twenty-five thousand on you to whip Dun Caffrey."

You know, I thought he'd gone crazy. I looked up at him and listened to him say it again.

Twenty-five thousand! Why, that was—it was impossible, that's what it was.

"They were ready for me," he said. "After all, this is a business with them. I mentioned having a fighter, and they doubted it—said nobody would stand a chance with Caffrey. Then they kept egging me on until they told me to put my money where my mouth was. And I did."

"Doc, for that much money they'd murder fifty like us. I won't fight. Tell 'em the bet's off."

"I can't...they made me put up the money. They've got me over a barrel."

The Bishop...he would have a gang ready to tear down the ropes and mob us if it looked as if I was going to win. He would be ready for us.

"They put up their money too, didn't they?"

"Of course." Halloran paced the floor. "Sackett, if I lose this bet I'll be back punching cows. It's everything I've been able to earn or save in forty-five years. I don't think I could do it again, and I can't imagine how I was such a fool."

I got up. "Don't let it worry you. I'll fight him. I'll beat him, too. But we've got to get somebody to guard that saloon safe, if that's where the money is. If there's no other way, they'll rob the safe."

"That's just it. The Bishop has men in town. He has several who have agreed to stay in the saloon and keep watch. Sackett, we're through. We're whipped!"

There was a tap on the door, and I slid that Walch Navy out of my waistband.

"Open it," I said to Juana. "Just pull it open and stay out of the way."

She pulled the door open and a man stepped into the doorway. He was tall and very lean, with yellow eyes and gold rings in his ears. "'Lando," he said, "I figured it was you."

It was the Tinker.

NINE

He stepped into the room and closed the door carefully behind him. The room was dimly lit, with the flickering fire on the hearth and a candle burning. The dark shadows lay in the hollows of his cheeks, and I could see little more of him than the gleam of his eyes and the shine of the gold of his earrings.

"When I heard of a man with a racing mule," he said, "it had to be you."

He stepped up to me and thrust out his hand, and a feeling came into my throat so I couldn't speak. I was not a man with many friends, but I wanted the Tinker to be one of them.

"You're heavier," he said, "and by heaven, you're a man!"

When I'd introduced him around, we all sat down. Experience had not made me a trusting man, and we'd been apart for a spell of years. But he was my friend, I was sure of that, and right now I needed him.

"The mule can run," I said, "he can really scat."

"He'll need to." He shot me a shrewd look. "Do you know whose money is against you? The Bishop's, that's whose. The Bishop's money and Caffrey's. Your Caffrey isn't only a fighter, he's a gambler—and he's a big one. The Bishop and him, they're partners."

"You know about the fight?"

"It's talked about. This is an Irish town, and you know the Irish—they love a good fight with the knuckles."

"I'll have a little of my own back. I want the hide off him, but I want to break his pocket, too. With a Caffrey, that will hurt the worst."

The Tinker was silent for several minutes, and there was no sound in the room but an occasional crackle from the fireplace and the faint hiss of the coffee pot.

We sat still around the room—the Tinker with his long, narrow face and gold earrings, Doc Halloran standing and looking long, lean and serious, with the black eyes of Juana and Manuel in the background.

"Deckrow's in town," the Tinker said finally, glancing around at Juana. "He's looking for you."

"His daughter is with him?"

"They're going to San Antonio. There's a lawsuit over the estate." He looked at me. "Your father should be here tomorrow, your father and his wife."

"He married Gin?"

"Love match—from the start. He's in great shape again and looks fine; and Gin, she's beautiful as ever. But Franklyn Deckrow claims the estate through his wife, and he claims he bought up mortgages. I don't understand lawing, but that's the way of it. The trouble will be settled in either San Antonio or Austin, but they're going to San Antonio now, then on to Austin, I think."

"I'll have to be there," I said. "I've evidence to offer."

Juana looked at me, and fear showed in her eyes. "Does he know? Señor Deckrow, does he know?"

"He knows...my eyes were on him and he saw it."

"Then tomorrow, when you fight?"

Doc and the Tinker, they just looked at me, and I said, "Deckrow was with Herrara's and Cortina's men that night. It was he and nobody else who killed Jonas. Shot him dead. It was Deckrow who tipped them off that we had come into Mexico after gold—they were expecting us."

"He'll kill you. He'll have to."

Looking down at my big hands, I shrugged. "He'll try."

That night I lay long awake, watching the red glow of the coals and thinking back over my life, and it didn't add up to much. I'd set out to become rich in the western lands, but going after that LaFitte gold had been my ruin. Maybe even starting west with the Tinker had been the finish of me.

When this was over I would go on...there were other Sacketts out in New Mexico, near the town of Mora. I would go there.

There was nobody for me here. Pa had married Gin, and he would be thinking of another family, and rightly so. It was true that I had felt strongly about Gin, but the physical needs of a man speak loud with a woman like her about, and there doesn't have to be anything else between you—although she was a man's woman in so many ways, and not only of the bed.

When I found a woman of my own, I hoped she would be like Gin. She and pa—I had seen it right off. They were for each other.

Me? Who was there for me? I was a man with nothing. A man with great shoulders and tremendous power in his hands, but nothing else. I owned a horse taken from horse thieves, and a mule bred by stealth, and nothing at all of which I could be proud. It was little enough I had in the way of learning, and in my mid-twenties I'd laid no foundation for anything.

Tomorrow there would be a horse race and then a fight, and with luck I should win one or both. Yet then there would remain the matter of surviving to enjoy my winnings. Horse-racing and fighting, these are not things upon which a man can build a useful life.

Tomorrow I would meet Dun Caffrey in the ring, with

my fists. He was a skilled fighter, and I was only one with great strength and good but long-unpracticed training. If I whipped Caffrey, I'd have some of my own back; and if I could settle the matter of Deckrow and live, then I'd go west and start again as I had wished to do.

One thing I had learned in these years: I could now speak Spanish. Somewhere, at sometime in the future, it might help.

Westward I had come to grow rich in the land, but six years had passed and I had no more than at the beginning.

At last I slept, and when I awakened day had come and the coals were smoldering, with only a faint glow of red here and there. The room was empty.

Clasping my hands behind my head, I tried to organize a day that would not organize, for there were too many factors outside my grasp. Before the day was over I would have repaid Dun Caffrey what I owed him, or would have taken a fearful beating. But the greatest danger lay not in losing, but in winning. In losing I would take a beating; in winning, there was every chance I might be shot.

The Tinker and Halloran came in together. "The race will be run at ten o'clock," Halloran said. "The course is all laid out—one half-mile from a standing start."

"All right."

"The fight will be at one o'clock. Eighteen-foot ring. It's all set up in the stock corral. Those who cannot get up to the ring will find a seat on the fence."

"How many horses in the race?"

"Five, including your mule. Nobody thinks a mule can run, except a few who came in from Oakville. Right now the betting is seven to one against your mule."

From my shirt pocket I took forty dollars, every cent I had in the world. "At those odds, or anything close," I said, "you bet it on the race. If we win, bet whatever's in hand on the fight.

"Meanwhile," I said, "I'm going to take a walk around."

This here town of Beeville, along about the time we were there—you could walk three blocks in any direction and be out in the country. And some of those blocks you'd walk would be mighty sparse as to buildings.

It was a cattle-trail town and ran long to saloons and gambling houses. The folks who lived in the country around were mostly raising cattle. The rest of them were stealing cattle. Both industries were in what you might call a flourishing condition when we came into town. There was considerable money floating about town, and not an awful lot to do with it but drink or gamble. When it came to ranching, there were several successful men around Beeville; but in the cattle-rustling business the most successful man was Ed Singleton.

The town was about evenly divided between the ranchers and the thieves, and each knew the others by name and occupation. You could hang a cattle thief back in those days, but the trouble was you had to catch him at it. Singleton and those others, they were almighty sly.

There was a lot of betting on both the fight and the race, some of the folks even betting on me, sight unseen. There's folks will bet on anything, given a chance.

Quite a crowd was in town. Some, like I said, had come over from Oakville, but there was a whole crowd from Helena, too. Helena was an old stop on the Chihuahua trail and, like Beeville and Oakville, it was a rough, wild town, and those men from Helena were as tough as they come.

I walked down the street, keeping away from the knots of men arguing here and there, and finally I stopped by the corral to look at that ring. It looked big enough, and small enough, too.

A man stopped beside me, looking through the corral bars at the ring. He glanced at me out of a pair of hard, measuring eyes, and thrust out his hand, "Walton. I'm sheriff. You fought much?"

"When I had to. Never in a contrivance like that."

"He's an experienced man, and a brute. I've seen him fight." He paused. "You must think you can beat him."

"A man never knows," I said, "but when we were kids I broke his nose and his jaw. I outsmarted him that time," I said, "maybe I can again."

"This a grudge fight?"

"If it isn't, then you never saw one. His pa used to beat me, and he robbed me. This one tried to bully me around. I figure he knows a lot more about fighting than I do, but I figure there's a streak of coyote in him. It may be mighty hard to find, but I'm going in there hunting it."

Walton straightened up. "There's fifty to a hundred thugs in town that nobody can account for without considering the Bishop. I'll do what I can, but I can't promise you anything."

"In this country," I said, "a man saddles his own broncos and settles his own difficulties."

Walton walked away, and after a bit I went back to the house and saddled the roan. Time was shaping up for the race.

Manuel had led the mule out. "They want to know his name," he said.

"What did you call him?"

Manuel shrugged.

"All right, call him Bonaparte, and let's hope that track out there isn't Waterloo."

The Tinker came out and mounted up, and Doc Halloran too. One of the others who showed up was a husky Irishman with a double-barreled shotgun.

"I'm a mule-skinner," he said, "and I bet on him. In my time I've seen some fast mules, and I saw this one run over to Oakville."

The Bishop was out there, and Dun Caffrey. I noticed they had at least two horses in the race.

"Manuel," I said, "how mean can you be?"

He looked at me from those big dark eyes. "I do not know, señor. I have never been mean."

"Then you've got only one chance. Get that mule out in

130

front and let him run. Those two"—I indicated the horses—
"are both ridden by tough men. One or both of them will try
to block you out if you look like you'd a chance, so watch
out."

"I will ride Bonaparte," he said—"it is all I can do, but
it is a proud name."

They lined up, and the way Bonaparte walked up to the
line you wouldn't have thought he'd anything in mind but
sleep. One of those Bishop horses moved in on each side of
him.

So I walked across to the Bishop. I walked up to him
right in front of everybody. "Tinhorn," I said, "you better
hope those boys of yours don't hurt that kid. If they do, I'll
kill you."

He thought it was big talk, but he made a little move
with his head and two husky shoulder-strikers moved up to
me. "Caffrey will kill you," the Bishop said, his voice deeper
than any I'd ever heard, "but these can rough you up a little
first."

One of them struck at me, and the Tinker's training was
instinctive. Grabbing his wrist, I busted him over my back
into the dust, and he came down hard. Coming up in a crouch,
the other man missed a blow and I saw the glint of brass
knuckles on his hand. My left hand grabbed his shirt collar
in front and took a sharp twist that set him to gagging and
choking. With the other I grabbed his hand, forcing his arm
up so that everybody within sight could see those brass
knuckles.

Now, like I've said, I was an uncommon strong man
before those years in prison. My fingers wrapped around his
hand just above the wrist and began to squeeze, squeezing
his fingers right up to a point, then I brought his hand down
and let those knuckle dusters fall into the dust. At the same
time I slipped my hand up a little further and shut down hard
with all my grip.

He screamed, a hoarse, choking scream. And then I put

131

my thumb against the base of his fingers and my fingers at his wrist and bent it back sharply. Folks standing nearby heard it break. Then I walked out to Manuel.

"You ride it clean, kid," I said. I spoke loud enough so all could hear. "If either of these make a dirty ride, they'll get what he got."

Somebody cheered, and then the pistol was fired.

Those horses taken out of there at a dead run, most of them cutting horses and expert at starting from a stand.

My mule, he was left at the post.

They just taken off and went away from there, but Manuel was figuring right. He held the mule back, and sure enough, those two riders to right and left crashed together. They had risked what I'd do rather than what the Bishop might do. If Manuel had been in there, he'd have been hurt, and bad.

Then Manuel let out a shrill whoop and that Bonaparte left out of there like he had some place to go and it was on fire.

He was two lengths behind before he made his first jump, but I'd never realized the length of his legs before. He had a tremendous stride, and he ran—he ran like no horse I'd ever seen.

There was no way for me to see the finish. It was a straightaway course, and several of them seemed to be bunched up at the end.

Suddenly one of the judges, a man on a white horse, came galloping back. "That damned mule!" he yelled. "The mule won by half a length!"

Back at the Mexicans' cabin nobody had much to say. The Mexican folks who owned it stayed out of sight most of the time and Juana stayed with them. I had made a bit of money and Halloran cut me in on what he'd made on the race, as well as giving a bit to Manuel. That I did too.

Those two races had made that boy more money than he and Juana had seen since Miguel died.

Me, I stretched out on the bed and lay there, resting up

for the fight. My stomach felt empty and kind of sick-like, and I began to wonder if I was scared. True enough, I'd whipped Caffrey, but he was no fighter then, just a big, awkward boy, and I might have been lucky. Now he had been out among men, he had proved himself against known fighters, defeating them all, and there's no escaping the worth of experience.

Between bouts he'd had a-plenty of sparring with experienced fighters, and was up to all manner of tricks that only a professional can come by. But I thought of Jem Mace, who'd taught the Tinker. He had been a master boxer, one of the great ones. Never weighing more than one hundred and sixty pounds, he had been the world's champion, defeating men as much as sixty pounds heavier.

Thinking about it, I dozed off and did not wake up until the Tinker shook me.

"Move around," he advised. "Get the sleep out of you. Get your blood to circulating."

O'Flaherty, the Irishman who'd bet on our mule, came to the house. "I've not seen you with the knuckles," he commented, "but a man with sense enough to bet on a mule is a canny one, so I bet my winnings on you."

The Tinker was carrying a pistol, a rare thing for him, and the Irishman had brought his shotgun. Doc Halloran had bulges under his coat that meant he was wearing two guns, and I slipped mine into my waistband, too.

We mounted up and started for the ring, but I'd gone no way at all when someone called out to me, and when I turned I saw it was a girl in a handsome carriage. It was Marsha Deckrow, and she was more beautiful than I would have believed anybody could be.

Pulling up, I removed my hat. "Still the servants' entrance?" I said.

She showed her dimples. "I was a child then, Orlando. I must have sounded very snippy."

"You did."

"You're stern!" She laughed at me. "I'm sorry you were in prison. My father told me about it."

133

"I must be going on," I said, though to be honest it was the last thing I wished to do.

"You're going to fight that awful man. My father won't let me go, even though I promised to sit in the carriage and we needn't be close. There's a knoll a little way from the corral, and we could keep the carriage there. But I'll watch. I think I've found a window."

"It is likely to be brutal," I said, "and he may whip me."

"Will I see you afterward, Orlando? After all, we're cousins, aren't we? Or something like that? Your father married my aunt."

"Do you see them often?"

"With your father feeling the way he does about pa? I should say not! In fact, we're on our way to Austin now."

I gathered the reins. The Tinker and Doc were waiting impatiently, and the time was soon. "You tell your pa for me," I said, "that he'd better drop that case. He'd best forget the whole thing. He was working for Jonas in the beginning, and when this is over he won't even be doing that."

Her face hardened. "You're my enemy then?"

"I'm not anybody's enemy," I said, "but I know murder when I see it done. And betrayal, too."

The look in her eyes there for a minute—well, it wasn't what you'd rightly call pleasant; but then it was gone and she was all smiles. "After the fight, Orlando? Win or lose? Will you come? Pa wouldn't approve, not one bit, but if you'd come to see me...I'm staying with the Appletons, down at the end of the street. They hadn't room for pa, too, so he won't be there. Do come."

"Well"—she was a mighty pretty girl—"I'll see."

My stomach felt queasy when I dismounted at the corral, for there were a sight of folks sitting atop the corral fence, which had a board nailed on it all the way around so's men could look at stock when buying from the corral.

Inside, the yard had been sprinkled and then rolled or tamped until it was hard-packed. They'd set four posts in the ground and had ropes around them, running through holes in the posts.

No sooner had I got down than a great yell went up from the crowd, and there was Dun Caffrey getting out of a carriage. He wore a striped sweater, and when he peeled it off, he showed a set of the finest shoulders a man ever did see.

He was some taller than me, maybe about three inches, and had longer arms. He would weigh better than me, for I was down to two hundred and six, whilst he weighed two hundred and thirty, and carrying no fat.

Folks crowded around—men in buckboards and spring wagons, men a-horseback and afoot.

Caffrey was wearing a pair of dark blue tights and some fancy, special-made shoes for boxing or handball. I wore moccasins and black tights—these last the Tinker rustled up for me.

"They've got a set of gloves," Doc Halloran said, "and they offer to fight either way, with or without."

"Take 'em," the Tinker advised. "They protect your hands, and you'll hit even harder because of them. A lot of folks don't realize it, but a man hits harder with a bandaged hand and a glove than with a bare fist—more compact, better striking surface, and less danger of hurting your hands."

When we agreed, they brought a pair of gloves over and I shoved my hand down inside. These were three-ounce gloves, and when my hand was doubled into a fist it was hard as rock.

"We fight London Prize Ring rules," Doc explained. "You fight until one man goes down, a knockdown, slip, or throw down, then you rest for one minute, and you toe the mark when you come up for each round, and the fight is to a finish."

"He knows," the Tinker said, dryly. He looked at me. "I hope you haven't forgotten what I taught you during those months of travel. You can use a rolling hip-lock to throw him, and if you get hold of him, pound him until you're stopped."

135

Everybody had been taking notice of Caffrey, and when I slipped off my sweater, nobody was looking my way. I was brown as any Indian, and there were the scars of the old whip-cuts on my back and shoulders.

In spite of the difference in weight between us, I was better muscled and a little broader in the shoulders and quite a bit thicker through the chest.

Walton was to referee, and he made an announcement that he'd shoot the first man to come through the ropes or the first to try to tear down a post.

Around that ring those gamblers were gathered. Right off I could see that they'd outsmarted us, and the whole crowd against the ropes except right in my corner were his friends, and the men behind them were, too. My friends, and few enough of them there were, they were cut off, back some distance.

Suppose a whole rank started to move in on the ring? What would Walton do then?

Time was called and we walked out to toe the mark, and as soon as my toe touched it, Caffrey hit me. He hit me a straight left to the face, and it landed hard. I sprang at him, punching with both hands, and he moved around me like a cooper around a barrel. He hit me three times in the face without my landing a blow.

The crowd began to yell, and he came at me again, but this time I ducked my head against his chest and managed to hit him twice, short blows in the belly, before he put a headlock on me and threw me to my knees, ending the round.

When I walked back to my corner and sat on Halloran's knee, my lip was puffed from a blow, and there was a knot on my cheekbone. I'll give it to him. He could punch.

"Stay close to him," the Tinker whispered. "Keep your hands higher and your elbows in. Work on his body when you get the chance."

When time was called, Caffrey rushed from his corner and began punching with both hands. He hit me several times, almighty hard, but I got my head down against his chest again and hooked both hands hard to the belly. He tried to push me off then, but I stepped in fast and back-heeled him and he went down hard, ending the round.

As we went on it was nip and tuck, both of us punching hard. He was fast, and he was in good shape, and he moved well. The first six rounds were gone in fourteen minutes, but the seventh round lasted five minutes all by itself.

He'd pounded me about the head, but I wasn't really hurt. He'd drawn first blood—there was a trickle of it from my lip that had been cut against my teeth. He was unmarked, and the betting had gone up to three to one on Caffrey.

Opposite us a window had gone up in the second story of a house, and I could see a couple of women there, watching the fight. Another window in that same house was open, too, but nobody watched from it.

Round eight came up and I went out fast, slipped a left lead for my head and smashed him in the ribs. It taken his wind, and it shook him up. It was my first hard punch of the fight, and I think it surprised him. He backed off, studying me, and I stalked him. I made awkwardly as if to throw my right and he stepped in, hitting hard with his right.

My left arm was bent at the elbow, first at shoulder level, elbow near the hip, and I'd moved my left shoulder and hip over almost to the center line, while leaving my fist cocked where it was. As Caffrey threw that right, I let go with my left, letting it whip around, thrown by the tension built up by turning my shoulder forward and the weight behind it.

The blow struck high on his cheekbone and knocked him across the ring into the ropes. Eager hands shoved him back, but I was moving in on him and I struck him again with my left fist, but I was too eager with my right, and missed. He clinched and back-heeled me into the dirt, falling atop me and jerking his knee into my groin.

Throwing him off, I came up fast and mad, and hurt by that knee. He cocked his fist, and then Walton stepped in and stopped the round.

Twice after that he drove me into the ropes and once I

137

was hit from outside the ropes, hit hard just above the kidney. I turned to complain and he knocked me down...a clean knock-down.

The crowd was mad now. Arguments were starting all about us, and there were several fights going close to the ring, and one back beyond it. Once, wrestling in a clinch, I thought I saw movement at that empty window, and made up my mind to speak to Doc about it.

It was bloody fighting now. Moving in, I smashed him in the mouth with a right that split his lip and started the blood flowing. In a clinch he said hoarsely, "I'm going to kill you, Sackett! Right here in this ring, I'm going to kill you!"

"I broke your bones once," I replied, "and I'll do it again!"

Catching his left arm under mine, I threw him off balance and hit him twice in the belly before I let go. We moved together, punching with both hands, and outside the ropes the crowd was shouting and brawling. Nothing could be heard above the din. Deliberately, I still pounded away at his body, but his stomach and ribs were like rock. He cut a slit above my eye and knocked me into the ropes, and there someone struck me a stunning blow over the back of the head with something like a blackjack or sandbag.

Even as I fell, Caffrey rushed at me and struck me twice in the face. I fell forward, and was scarcely conscious as the Tinker and Doc dragged me to my corner. Yet when the bell rang I was on my feet.

Now he started after me, and, still feeling the effects of the blow over the head, I could not get myself together. My punches were poorly timed and lacked force, and Caffrey rushed at me, pounding away with both hands. Getting in close, I seized him bodily, lifted him clear of the ground, and slammed him down with such force that the wind was knocked from him.

"The one in the checked suit," Doc whispered, "he's the one who sapped you."

Glancing across the ring, I saw him there, a broad-faced man with coarse features, who was wearing a black hat.

Caffrey was wary of me now, and we circled a bit, and I backed him slowly toward the man in the checked suit. That man, I noticed, had his right hand out of sight under his coat. Near the ropes I moved in, feinted, ducked a left, and landed a right under the heart, pushing him back into the ropes. Smashing another blow to the belly, I deliberately pushed him against the ropes so the men crowded there must give way, then I struck hard at his head, but off aim just enough for the blow to miss, which it did.

It missed him, but it caught the man in the checked suit on his red, bulbous nose and smashed it, sending a shower of blood over him as he fell.

We slugged in mid-ring then, slugged brutally, taking no time, just punching away. The things that the Tinker had taught me were coming back now. I stabbed a straight left to the mouth, then crossed my right to his chin. He hit me with a solid right and I staggered, but as he closed in I clinched, caught his right elbow in my left hand, and my right arm went around his body. Then I turned my hip against him and hurled him heavily to the dirt.

He was slow getting up, and suddenly I felt better. There was a cut over my eye, a welt on my cheekbone I could scarcely see over, and my lip had been split, but I felt better. I had my second wind, and suddenly all the old feeling against the Caffreys was welling up inside me. They had robbed me and enslaved me, they had treated me cruelly when there was no chance to fight back. Now we would see.

When time was called I went out fast. I feinted and hit him with a solid right on the jaw. His knees buckled, so I moved in fast to catch him before he could fall and bull him into the ropes. If he went down he would have rest and might recover. Men tried to push him off the ropes so he could fall, but I held him there and hit him with both hands in the face with all the power I had.

When he started to fall away from the ropes I caught him with another punch, and then he did fall. Turning back to my corner, my eyes momentarily caught a flash of light. Involuntarily I ducked, but there was nothing. Glancing at the empty window, I found it still empty.

The gamblers were pushing hard on the ropes, and Sheriff Walton shouted at them to hold back, but they were pushing as a mass and there was no one he could single out for a shot, and he was not the man to fire blindly into a crowd.

When we came together again in the center of the ring, I said, "Dun Caffrey, you and your folks robbed me, now I shall have a little of my own back."

He cursed me, and beat me to the punch with a left that jolted me. There was power in the man. He was a fighter— I'll give him that.

The crowd was shouting wildly, their faces red with fury at me. They had not expected me to last so long, yet here I was, in danger of beating their man.

Sweat trickled into my eye and the salt stung, and, momentarily blinded, I failed to see the right with which he knocked me into the ropes. Now it was he who held me there, and as he battered at me with both fists, several men pounded the back of my head and my kidneys from beyond the ropes. Had they left it to one man he might have done me serious injury, but so eager were they, and most of them drinking, that they interfered with one another.

I got my head down against his chest and again the great strength of me helped, for I bulled him away from the ropes and into the center of the ring.

As we broke apart, each ready for a blow, sunlight flashed again in my eyes—sunlight reflected from a rifle barrel. In the window which until now had seemed empty, a man was aiming a rifle at me.

Wildly, I threw a punch at Caffrey, deliberately throwing myself forward and off balance so that I fell to the ground, but even as I fell I heard the *whap* of a rifle bullet as it whipped past me, and then I was on my hands and knees in the dirt and all about me there was silence.

Looking up, I saw the crowd drawing back. Slumped against a ring post was a man with a round blue hole over one eye and the back of his head blown away.

In that instant, the Bishop, never one to miss a chance, sprang into the ring holding up a watch and claiming I had been off my feet for the count of ten—that I had lost, I had been knocked out.

"No!" Walton shouted, and drawing his own gun, he said, "the fight will continue. May the best man win."

The thugs and gamblers crowded back again toward the ring, shouting angrily that the fight was ended, but before they could reach the ropes, a horse vaulted over them and a man with a shotgun sat in the saddle.

"Stand back from the ropes!" His voice seemed not to be lifted above a conversational tone, but it had the ring of authority. "We'll have no interference here."

The thugs stared at the shotgun and the man who held it, and hesitated, as well they might. Captain McNelly was not a man who spoke careless words.

"I would advise you," he said, "to look about you before any violence is attempted. I am McNelly, and the men you see are my company of Rangers. We will see fair play here, and no violence outside the ring."

Their heads turned slowly, unwilling to believe what they saw, but thirty mounted and armed men are a convincing sight, and I confess, it was pleased I was to see them.

McNelly spoke to his horse, which easily lifted itself over the ropes again. "Sheriff Walton," he said quietly, "whenever you are ready."

"*Time!*" Walton said, and stepped back.

It was a bloody bit of business that remained, for I found no streak of cowardice in Dun Caffrey. Many things he might have been, but there was courage in the man. He had had a few minutes of respite, and now he came up to the mark,

141

fresh as only a well-conditioned veteran can be. For the veteran knows better how to rate himself, how to make the other man do the work and exert himself; and Caffrey was prepared to give me a whipping.

But the fighting had served a purpose with me also. No veteran of many fights, nonetheless I had sparred much with the Tinker and he had shown me many things, and practiced me in their doing, and the fight thus far had served to bring them to mind.

So if it was a strong and skilled man I still faced, it was a different one he faced now.

My muscles were loose now, my body warmed up, and I was sweating nicely under the hot sun. The rhythm of punching had become more natural to me, and my mind was working in the old grooves.

As I came in more slowly, my mind was thinking back to what the Tinker had taught me. Caffrey shot a left for my face and, going under it, I hit him with a right to the heart, rolling inside of his right. I smashed my left to the ribs, then hooked a right to the head over his left.

The right landed solidly, and Caffrey blinked. Moving in, I shook him with another right and a left. For a long minute we slugged. I could feel the buzz in my head from his punches, the taste of blood from my split lip. I saw his fist start and brushed it aside, driving my right to his chin inside his left. He backed up, trying to figure it out, but whatever else he was, Caffrey was no thinking fighter. Weaving, I hit him with both hands.

Outside, the air was filled with sound, men were shouting, cheering, crying out with anger. Not with blood lust, but with the excitement of any dramatic thing—and what could be more dramatic than a fight like this one?

He hit me with a left, but the steam had gone from his punches. I tried a light left, watching for the move I wanted. And it came again, the same too-wide left he had tried only a moment before. Only that time my right caught him coming in. My fist struck solidly on the point of his chin, like the butt of an axe striking a log, and he fell face forward into the dirt.

For a moment there I stood looking down at him. This was the man whose father and mother had cheated me and robbed me, and who had gone on to riches on the money that should have been spent for my education, the education I'd always wanted. Yet, suddenly, I no longer felt any hatred, all of it washed clean in the trial of battle.

Stooping down, I picked him up and helped him to his corner, and as I stopped him there, where of a sudden there was nobody to receive him, his eyes opened and he looked around.

Me, I let go of him and held out my mitt. "It was a good fight, Dun. You're a tough man."

He blinked at me, then held out his own hand and we stood there looking surprised, like two fools.

And then I turned and walked away and leaned against the roan, which had been led up for me. The Tinker was handing me my sweater. "Get into this," he said; "you'll take cold."

Taking it from his hand, I said, "I got to see a man."

"The one who tried to kill you? He got away."

"No, he didn't."

We walked, the Tinker and me, along the dusty street. Doc Halloran walked behind us with Captain McNelly and Sheriff Walton.

Their rig was coming down the street toward us, and there for a moment I thought he was going to try to ride right over us, but he drew up and stopped when we stopped, barring his way.

Marsha was there in the seat beside her father, and nobody else with them. They were alone, those two, but somehow I had a feeling they'd always been alone.

Deckrow's face showed nothing, but it never had. His eyes looked at me, cold and measuring, with no give to them.

"You shot and killed your brother-in-law, Jonas Locklear," I said, "and it was you tipped Herrara off that we were in Mexico, and what for."

"I do not have any idea what you are speaking about," he replied, looking at me sternly. "I am sure I would be the last man to shoot my own brother-in-law."

"I saw you shoot him," I persisted, "and Miguel did also. That's why he died. That's why you tried to kill me today."

"You ought to be ashamed," Marsha said, "telling lies about my father."

You know something? I was sorry for him. He was a little man and nothing much had ever happened to him, and with all his planning and figuring he could never make any money; while Jonas, who did all the wrong things, was always making it. And now he had to pay for it all.

Trouble with me was, I was a mighty poor hater. There was satisfaction in winning, but winning would have been better if nobody had to lose. That's the way I've always felt, I guess.

Seems to me I'm the sort of man who, if a difficulty arose, might knock a man down and kick all his teeth out, but then would help him pick them up if he was so inclined, and might even pay the bill for fixing them—although that's going a bit far.

"That property," I said, "the ranch and the house and all, belongs to Gin and your wife, unless a will said otherwise...not to you.

"You've no claim"—I spoke louder to prevent his attempted interruption—"and you tried to get one through murder. I will take oath, here and now and in court, that you betrayed and then shot down your brother-in-law. Furthermore," I said, and lied when I said it, "I can get Mexicans to testify they saw it.

"You sign over all claims to Gin and your wife—"

"My wife left me," he said.

"You sign over all claims or I'll have you on trial for murder."

He sat there holding the lines and hating me, but he

hadn't much to say. The trouble was, he was a man with a canker for a soul, and he would be eaten away with his bitterness at failure, nor did I care much.

It is wrong to believe that such men suffer in the conscience for what they do...it is only regret at being caught that troubles them. And they never admit it was any fault of their own...it was always chance, bad luck....The criminal does not regret his crime, he only regrets failure.

The Bishop was standing by listening, but I paid him no mind. There had been a time when he seemed awesome and dangerous, but that was a while back.

"You remember what I said, Deckrow," I told him, "because wherever it is this is settled, San Antonio or Austin or wherever, I'll be there."

When I came up to the house pa was there, and Gin beside him. He looked fine...they were a handsome couple if I ever saw one—but I was sure I'd never get around to calling her ma.

I stepped down from the saddle and slid my Winchester from the boot, and pa looked at me. "Somebody gave you a beating," he said.

"He didn't give it to me," I replied, "I fought for it."

"You'll be coming with us now? I've held your share of the gold...it's been waiting your return."

"Buy something with it in my name. I'll come for it one day...or send a son of mine for it."

"You're going back for the rest?"

"When I left Tennessee for the western lands it was in my mind to become rich with the goods of this world, but by planning and trade, not by diving for dead men's gold. I shall go on to the West."

"You still want me along?" the Tinker asked.

"We left Tennessee together. I left with you and a mule. It's fitting we hold to our course. However, we never did make a dicker for one of your knives. Now, I'd give—"

"Stand aside, Gin," pa interrupted, "there's trouble."

When I turned around it put me alongside of pa, although

there was a space between us. And the Tinker stood off to one side of me.

And there facing us were the three Kurbishaws, three tall men in dusty black, Elam, Gideon, and Eli.

Pa was first to speak. "You've come a long way from Charleston, Elam...a long way."

"We came for you."

"You will find most of the gold still there...if you can get it," pa said coolly. "We've had ours."

"It isn't for gold anymore," Gideon said. "There's more to it."

"I suppose there is," pa replied, his voice still cold. "You hounded your sister to death; you hunted my son."

"And now we got him," Elam replied, "—and you."

Pa didn't want it, I could see that. He was talking to get out of it, to get it stopped, but they would not listen. Strange men they were, but I'd see their like again, in lynch mobs and elsewhere. They were men who knew what I did not—they knew how to hate.

"You wouldn't try me alone," pa said. "Now there's two of us."

"Three," said the Tinker.

"We've come a far piece since then," Elam said, "and we've lived as we might, by the gun."

"Why, then," pa said, "if you'll have it no other way—"

Gideon was looking at me, so when pa drew I swung up the muzzle of my Winchester and levered a shot into him. I saw the bullet dust him at the belt line, and worked the lever again and fired. He threw his gun hand high in a queer, dance-like gesture, and then he tried to bring it down on me. I stepped forward and shot again and my bullet went high, striking at the collarbone and tearing away part of his throat as it glanced off.

The sound of shooting was loud in the street, and then there was stillness, the acrid smell of gunpowder mixed with dust, and we three stood there, facing them as they lay. The last one alive was Eli, tugging at one of Tinker's knives sunk deep into his chest.

"If that's the only way," I commented, "to get one of those knives, I'll wait."

Looking down at them, I thought it was a strange trail they had followed, those three, and how in the end it had only come to this, to death in a dusty street, nobody caring; and by and by nobody even remembering, except by gossip over a bar in a saloon.

Seemed it was just as well a man did not know where he was headed when he was to come only to this—a packet of empty flesh and clothes to end it all. In the end their hatred had bought them only this...only this, and the bitter years between.

It always seemed that for me something waited in those western lands, something of riches in the way of land and living, and maybe a woman. And when I found her, I wanted her to be like Gin.

Younger, of course, as would be fitting, but like her.

Somebody likely to have no more sense than to fall in love with a Tennessee boy with nothing but his two hands and a racing mule.